He had a gash near his temple.

"Mister?" Louanne asked. "Are you all right?"

He didn't respond.

Was he unconscious? Or just drifting in and out?

She knelt and checked for a pulse, found it beating strong and steady.

The stranger opened his eyes—blue as the summer sky—and spoke. "No ambulance...no hospital. I'm...okay."

Louanne didn't believe him. Was he running from someone? Hiding out?

Like she was?

She supposed she ought to be worried about taking the battered stranger back to her house, but for some reason, she wasn't. Maybe because he appeared to be such an interesting contradiction. The kind of character who would fit nicely into the novel she'd been writing.

A handsome but rugged stranger.

Dangerous but vulnerable.

A hellion...with angel eyes...

Dear Reader,

It's that time of year again—back to school! And even if you've left your classroom days far behind you, if you're like me, September brings with it the quest for everything new, especially books! We at Silhouette Special Edition are happy to fulfill that jones, beginning with *Home on the Ranch* by Allison Leigh, another in her bestselling MEN OF THE DOUBLE-C series. Though the Buchanans and the Days had been at odds for years, a single Buchanan rancher—Cage—would do anything to help his daughter learn to walk again, including hiring the only reliable physical therapist around. Even if her last name did happen to be Day....

Next, THE PARKS EMPIRE continues with Judy Duarte's *The Rich Man's Son,* in which a wealthy Parks scion, suffering from amnesia, winds up living the country life with a single mother and her baby boy. And a man passing through town notices more than the *passing* resemblance between himself and newly adopted infant of the local diner waitress, in *The Baby They Both Loved* by Nikki Benjamin. In *A Father's Sacrifice* by Karen Sandler, a man determined to do the right thing insists that the mother of his child marry him, and finds love in the bargain. And a woman's search for the truth about her late father leads her into the arms of a handsome cowboy determined to give her the life her dad had always wanted for her, in *A Texas Tale* by Judith Lyons. Last, a man with a new face revisits the ranch—and the woman—that used to be his. Only, the woman he'd always loved was no longer alone. Now she was accompanied by a five-year-old girl...with very familiar blue eyes....

Enjoy, and come back next month for six complex and satisfying romances, all from Silhouette Special Edition!

Gail Chasan
Senior Editor

Please address questions and book requests to:
Silhouette Reader Service
U.S.: 3010 Walden Ave., P.O. Box 1325, Buffalo, NY 14269
Canadian: P.O. Box 609, Fort Erie, Ont. L2A 5X3

The Rich Man's Son

JUDY DUARTE

SPECIAL EDITION®

Published by Silhouette Books

America's Publisher of Contemporary Romance

Special thanks and acknowledgment are given to Judy Duarte for her contribution to THE PARKS EMPIRE series.

To Crystal Green and Sheri WhiteFeather, who always go above and beyond the call of critique partner duty. Your dedication, support and friendship mean the world to me. Without you, I might still be laboring over Chapter Twelve. Thank you, ladies, from the bottom of my heart.

And to my daughter, Christy Freetly, who took time to look over this book in manuscript form. Thanks for the thumb's-up. I love you, T.

SILHOUETTE BOOKS

ISBN 0-373-24634-X

THE RICH MAN'S SON

Copyright © 2004 by Harlequin Books S.A.

Visit Silhouette Books at www.eHarlequin.com

Printed in U.S.A.

JUDY DUARTE,

an avid reader who enjoys a happy ending, always wanted to write books of her own. One day, she decided to make that dream come true. Five years and six manuscripts later, she sold her first book to Silhouette Special Edition.

Her unpublished stories have won the Emily and the Orange Rose awards, and in 2001 she became a double Golden Heart finalist. Judy credits her success to Romance Writers of America and two wonderful critique partners, Sheri WhiteFeather and Crystal Green, both of whom write for Silhouette.

At times, when a stubborn hero and a headstrong heroine claim her undivided attention, she and her family are thankful for fast food, pizza delivery and video games. When she's not at the keyboard or in a Walter Mitty–type world, she enjoys traveling, spending romantic evenings with her personal hero and playing board games with her kids.

Judy lives in Southern California and loves to hear from her readers. You may write to her at: P.O. Box 498, San Luis Rey, CA 92068-0498. You can also visit her Web site at www.judyduarte.com.

THE PARKS EMPIRE

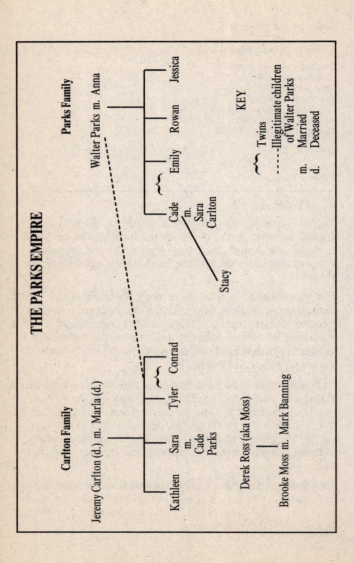

Parks Family

Walter Parks m. Anna

Cade ⎰ Emily   Rowan   Jessica
m.
Sara
Carlton

Stacy

Carlton Family

Jeremy Carlton (d.) m. Marla (d.)

Kathleen   Sara   Tyler   Conrad
           m.
           Cade
           Parks

Derek Ross (aka Moss)

Brooke Moss m. Mark Banning

KEY

⎰ Twins

------ Illegitimate children of Walter Parks

m.   Married
d.   Deceased

Chapter One

"Want some company?"

Rowan Parks looked up from his long-necked bottle of beer and caught the appreciative smile of a bleached-blond cowgirl in a red, low-cut blouse that threatened to pop a button if she took a deep breath.

"Afraid not." He motioned for the waitress, indicating he wanted to close out his tab and get on his way to nowhere in particular.

The blonde took a seat across from him anyway, put her elbows on the table and leaned forward. "My name's Charlene."

Rowan didn't respond. Women often sidled up to him in a bar with the intention of warming his bed. But sex was the furthest thing from his mind this evening.

And so was company.

"What's your name?" she asked, not at all put off by his silence.

Rowan wasn't up for this. He'd been stewing in his anger and his grief for days. And he wasn't ready for a change of mood. Nor was he willing to knock off the chip that weighed heavily upon his shoulder.

It felt too damn good to be miserable. Especially in a seedy little hole-in-the-wall like this.

Brenda Wheeler, his father's housekeeper and the woman who'd raised him and his siblings, had always made a big deal about being courteous. Polite.

But Rowan couldn't see any point in being honest. He glanced at the wood-paneled room, caught a whiff of stale beer and tobacco. Listened as an old country western song boomed from a red-and-chrome jukebox—Hank Williams at his best.

The tune wafted through the air like a curl of cigarette smoke, giving Rowan a quick and easy pseudonym. "My name is Hank."

Her blue eyes lit up, and she smiled, revealing a chipped front tooth. "Hank? No kidding? Just like the singer?"

He nodded, wishing the waitress would hurry up. The Watering Hole had been nearly empty when he'd first parked his Harley outside, trudged up the graveled walk and took a seat in the far corner, hoping to quench his thirst and wash the dust from his throat. But as more and more locals began to fill the wooden tables and red-vinyl corner booths, their laughter and Southern twangs played havoc with his sullen mood.

The blonde, Charlene, glanced at the diamond stud he wore in one ear, the platinum Rolex on his wrist, then studied his face with a good deal more interest than he wanted to cultivate.

"You're not from around here, are you?"

She had that right.

Rowan was as out of place in this Texas honky-tonk as he'd always been in the San Francisco mansion in which he'd grown up. But he didn't see any reason to comment. He wasn't into chitchat. Or revelations of his hell-bent flight to anonymity and peace.

When the waitress brought his check, he reached into his jeans pocket, pulled out a roll of cash wrapped in a rubber band, withdrew a twenty-dollar bill and set it on the brown Formica tabletop.

"Things really get hoppin' around here on Friday nights," Charlene said, offering him a friendly grin. "And the band will be settin' up pretty soon."

Rowan wasn't interested in boot scootin' or two-steppin', and the only mood music he felt like listening to was the blues. But something told him he wouldn't find a darkened jazz club out in the sticks.

"The band is really good. In fact, they've even had gigs in Austin. I know, 'cause my brother plays steel guitar." She tried to urge a smile from him, but it didn't work. "You're not going to up and walk away, are you?"

That's *exactly* what he was going to do. And it was

exactly what he'd done a couple of days ago—he'd walked away for good. And right now he only wanted to be left alone.

"Has anyone ever said that you look like Antonio Banderas?" she asked, apparently not giving up. Not used to being ignored.

Blessed with black hair, deep-set dimples and blue eyes, Rowan was the only one in the whole family to inherit his mother's ability to stop people in their tracks because of his good looks.

It had been a double-edged sword, though, since he'd had a feeling it was his physical resemblance to his mother that caused his father to shun him.

"I like the look of a five o'clock shadow on a man," Charlene said. "It makes y'all look kind of dangerous and sexy."

And rebellious, Rowan supposed. His refusal to shave every day had really irritated his old man. So had his troublemaking. But at least his rebellion had finally finagled a reaction out of his father.

You ungrateful bastard. Why can't you be more like your brother, Cade?

And less like your mother, Rowan had always internally supplied.

Was that what made his dad ignore him? The fact that Rowan looked like the woman his father had committed to a sanitarium in Switzerland?

Or had the jewelry baron merely found Rowan lacking?

Either way, as the black sheep of the family, Rowan had done everything he could to rebel against his father, a man who'd shown his ruthless side one time too many.

And now Rowan was out to shed his roots and prove himself. He'd never been one to pretend to be something he wasn't, to follow the crowd or to blend into the woodwork. But the problem was, he'd been keeping his pain and his dreams a secret for so long, that even *he* wasn't sure who *he* really was.

"Cat got your tongue?" Charlene asked.

"I'm just passing through. And as pretty as you are, Charlene, I'm not in the mood for conversation." He slid her a half smile that didn't reach his eyes. "Thanks for the company."

Then he sauntered out of the bar with his helmet under his arm. But instead of wearing it, he strapped it to the side of the bike, revved the engine and sped away, letting the wind blow through his hair and hoping it would clear his mind, his heart. His soul.

The Harley kicked up dust as Rowan raced down a country road. He had no idea where he was heading, other than as far away from the mighty Parks Empire as he could get. He'd been riding aimlessly for days, hoping to find some peace—away from the spider of a man who tried to keep his family and everyone else within his web of control.

Having made only brief, overnight stops from his trek, Rowan had grown tired of the reckless pace and decided to find a decent place to spend the night.

Where the hell was the interstate? He would need to head toward Austin to find something more than a run-down motel with a surging neon light that advertised Vacancy.

As the bike picked up speed, a jackrabbit dashed across the road, a coyote on its tail. Rowan swerved to avoid the mangy dog-like critter, and the Harley skidded into a deep gully that ran along an expansive string of worn-out barbwire fence.

When the bike hit the ditch, it bucked like a mechanical bull, throwing Rowan into the air.

He expected the raw pain upon impact, as flesh and bone met dirt, rocks and fencing. Even getting the wind knocked out of his chest hadn't really surprised him.

But he hadn't anticipated a fade to black.

Louanne Brown hated the Lazy B Ranch—always had and always would. But as fate would have it, the place she'd always been ashamed of had become a miracle when she'd needed it most.

Still, the never-ending chores began before dawn and continued nonstop until after supper. And at night, when she finally slipped between the clean but worn sheets of the hundred-year-old bed that had once belonged to her parents, she collapsed into an exhausted, bone-weary slumber.

Yet in spite of the calluses, the chapped hands and reddened knuckles, she whispered a prayer of thanksgiving that she and her sister hadn't put the ranch on the market after her folks died. And that Pete and Aggie Robertson had agreed to stay on, even though they'd reached retirement age.

The older couple had lived on the ranch for nearly as long as Louanne could remember and had become more than the foreman and his wife. They were surrogate grandparents to her son and friends to her. Friends who didn't pry. They'd noticed that she'd cloistered herself on the property, but hadn't said too much about it.

As the white, beat-up Ford pickup bounced along the potholes in the country road that surrounded the cattle ranch, she squinted in the late morning sunlight, her arm resting along the window of the passenger side. She'd been up since before daybreak, fixed a hearty breakfast for herself and given Noah a morning bottle before taking him to Aggie, who would care for the baby until Louanne came in for the noon meal.

"Here's that stretch of fence that needs mending," Pete said, from behind the wheel. "We really need to replace the whole blasted thing."

Imagine that. Every time Louanne turned around, she was met with one expense or another. "It's an ongoing battle to stay on top, isn't it?"

Pete nodded and clicked his tongue. "Sure seems that way."

Louanne didn't respond. She didn't need to.

Money had always been tight, more so now than ever. And there was no way they could splurge on something that major, no matter how sound the investment.

"Well, I'll be go-to-hell." Pete pointed to the northwest. "Look over there."

Louanne, following his direction, spotted a dark-haired man wandering along the road, dazed and battered. "He's hurt, Pete. Pull over."

When the pickup stopped, Louanne opened the door and slid out the passenger side. But before either of them could reach the wounded stranger, he crumpled to the ground.

His hair was caked in dried blood, probably coming from the gash near his temple. A dirty, white T-shirt bore blood spatters, and faded jeans sported a frayed rip in the knee.

A single diamond earring and a heavily bristled beard made him look like a rock musician or maybe an artist—just the kind of guy her sister Lula would date.

"Mister?" Louanne asked. "Are you all right?"

He didn't respond.

Was he unconscious? Or just drifting in and out?

She knelt and checked for a pulse, found it beating strong and steady.

Pete stood to the side, blocking the sun and casting a shadow on the man. "Maybe we ought to take him back to the ranch, then call an ambulance."

The stranger opened his eyes—blue as the summer sky—and shook his head. "No ambulance…no hospital. I'm…okay."

Louanne didn't believe him. He was obviously hurt. So why didn't he want medical treatment?

Was he running from someone? Hiding out?

Like she was?

She decided to honor his request—if possible.

"Are you able to climb in the back of the truck?" Pete asked him.

The man nodded, then slowly got to his feet. His knees seemed to buckle, so Pete and Louanne stood at his side to offer their support.

She supposed she ought to be worried about taking the battered stranger back to the house, but for some reason, she wasn't. Maybe because he appeared to be such an interesting contradiction. The kind of character who would fit nicely into the novel she'd been writing.

A handsome but rugged stranger.

Dangerous and vulnerable.

A hellion with angel eyes.

Even the clothes and accessories he wore mocked one another—the expensive platinum Rolex, faded denim jeans torn at the knee and dusty, leather boots that must have cost a pretty penny.

Of course, looks could be deceiving. Louanne had learned that the hard way. Still, she couldn't very well leave the injured stranger to the elements.

"Be careful," she told Pete, as they helped him into

the back of the pickup. Once he was sprawled out on the dirty, work-worn, metal bed, Louanne climbed in beside him.

On the bumpy ride back to the house, the man opened his eyes and searched her face. "What happened?"

"I was going to ask you the same thing." She mustered a smile, trying hard not to lose herself in his deep blue gaze. She had a feeling many women found it hard not to stare when he was clean and freshly shaven. In fact, she had a hard time keeping her eyes from settling on the angular jaw, the bristled cheeks. The spike of thick, black lashes seen only in a mascara commercial.

"Where am I?" he asked.

"At a ranch in Pebble Creek."

He grimaced, furrowing his brow—a near perfect brow, except for an old scar that tweaked his left eyebrow. He'd have another scar now. Higher. Near the temple. "Pebble Creek? Where the hell is that?"

"About an hour or two from Austin."

"Texas?"

She nodded.

He snagged her gaze with those baby blues, then reached out his hand and caught her wrist. "I'm glad you found me."

The warmth of his touch stirred up a flutter in her stomach, a reaction she hadn't had in nearly two years and hadn't expected to ever have again. "I'm glad, too. This road isn't very well traveled, so you might have had a long wait."

He searched her hair, her eyes, her face, as though looking for something. "I'm sorry. But I don't remember your name."

She wanted to say Lanay Landers, the name she'd created as a teenager and used while in college, but the name had died, along with her dreams. Instead, she told him the simple, unadorned truth. "Louanne Brown."

He nodded, as though it suited her. And the fact that he thought it had twisted inside her heart.

Hadn't her sister been the one to initiate the dream by insisting the key to a new life was in finding a new identity? Lula created a stage name, calling herself Tallulah Brown. And it had worked. She was now an up-and-coming starlet in Hollywood.

But fate hadn't been as kind to Louanne. And the pen name she'd planned to use now hid in a darkened corner of the closet, along with the manuscript that would never again see the light of day.

"You look familiar," the wounded man said. "Like I should know you."

She wished she could say the same. The handsome, raven-haired stranger didn't look like anyone she'd ever known. Or anyone she'd ever meet in Pebble Creek—better known as Nowhere, Texas.

Back east, when she was a graduate student in English, people used to think she looked familiar. But she'd dressed differently then, worn her hair in a loose, shoulder-length style.

Richard Keith, the college professor who had fathered Noah, always said Louanne looked a bit like Cindy Crawford, only not quite as glamorous. She also resembled her sister, who was becoming more and more well-known. But with each step Tallulah Brown inched toward superstardom, Louanne seemed to slip backward.

Her once promising literary career was over before it even had a chance to begin.

Mr. Enigma closed his eyes before she could ask him his name. But there was plenty of time for that, she supposed.

Pete parked near the house, then climbed from the truck and peered at the injured man, assessing him. Louanne couldn't be sure whether he was trying to make a judgment on his character or his wounds. Both, she supposed.

"His injuries could be serious," Pete told her. "We probably ought to take him to the city."

Louanne had been avoiding Austin because Richard would focus his search for her there. For that reason, she'd remained low-key, not leaving the ranch, not even going into Pebble Creek for groceries. Instead, she allowed Aggie to do the shopping.

Call her paranoid, but she wasn't eager to draw attention to herself by calling for an ambulance or filing a police report.

"Why don't we let Doc Haines come out and take a look at him?" she asked Pete.

The foreman nodded. "Sounds like a good idea. Doc might be getting on in years, but he knows his stuff."

Thank God for that. The country physician who still made house calls had not only delivered Noah, he'd provided her son's pediatric checkups and immunizations, too.

Once Doc had suggested Louanne go to a younger doctor in the city, but she refused, explaining that she wanted her son to have the same quality care she'd had as a child.

There was more to it, of course. Much more.

But the nightmare she'd experienced at the small eastern college was a secret she would keep to herself.

Before either Louanne or Pete could ponder how to get the injured man from the truck into the house, he stirred again. "Where am I?"

"You're at the Lazy B Ranch."

"Where's that?"

"Texas," she repeated.

He'd already asked that question. Had he forgotten? Or was he confused and suffering from a concussion?

Head injuries could be very serious. Maybe she ought to reconsider and have Pete drive him to the hospital. God forbid the man up and die on her. "Maybe we can transport you to an ER in Austin."

The man shook his head. "No hospital. Just let me get some rest, and I'll be okay."

"Can you walk into the house?" she asked, hoping that she and Pete, who had a bum knee, wouldn't have to carry him up the porch steps and down the hall.

He nodded, then slowly sat up and climbed from the truck. Louanne and Pete helped him into the house, but by the time they reached the spare room, he wobbled on his feet.

"I don't know about this, Louanne." Pete scrunched his craggy face and adjusted the weathered Stetson he rarely removed. "You better go call Doc Haines and let him decide what to do with this feller."

Pete was probably right. What was she going to do with a stranger in her spare room?

She hoped Doc would take over from here. Maybe he could have the man airlifted to the hospital, which would leave Louanne out of the limelight.

The stranger glanced at the crocheted coverlet on the bed that had once been Lula's and sighed heavily. "I'll get it dirty."

Louanne pulled back the bedding, revealing white cotton sheets that had been bleached by the sun while hanging on the clothesline to dry. "Sit here so Pete and I can take off your boots."

"We better take off more than that," Pete said, looking at the dirty jeans and bloody shirt.

Undress him? Louanne froze in her tracks. The man's devilish good looks stirred the feminine feelings she'd long since buried—after her baby's father made her fear for her life.

"I need a shower," he said.

Well, Pete with his bum knee wouldn't be able to support him.

"Maybe we ought to wait until the doctor gets here," Louanne said. If Doc decided to take him to the city, undressing the man would be someone else's responsibility.

Yet for some crazy reason, she felt a bit disappointed handing the chore over to someone else.

His head hurt like hell. And each time he opened his eyes, the ache seemed to grow worse. But he didn't complain. In fact, he didn't do anything but try not to be stiff and unyielding while the woman—Louanne—removed his shirt. Her hands were roughened from work, yet gentle.

She looked familiar, like he really ought to know her. But for the life of him, he couldn't figure out who she was. Maybe it was those golden-brown eyes that seemed to peer deep inside of him.

As she wiped his face, the wet, warm cloth scratched against the bristles of his beard, making him wish he'd shaved this morning.

Her scent was something earthy and floral, something he hadn't ever smelled before. Something kind of nice.

Unable to help himself, he opened his eyes again,

trying to catch another glimpse of her, giving himself a chance to remember where he'd seen her before—if he actually had.

Her brows, delicate arches of brown, furrowed as she ministered to him. And when she glanced up and spotted him looking at her, her breath caught. "Am I hurting you?"

"No."

"Good." Their gazes held a bit longer than necessary, then she dipped the washcloth into the warm water and wrung it out. "Can you sit up? I'd like to remove your shirt."

He nodded, then pushed himself forward. Slipping a T-shirt over his head was an easy chore, but he wasn't sure he could have managed without her help.

"You make a great nurse," he said, trying to lighten the mood. Trying to stay on an even keel.

"Thank you." She continued wiping him down, and he found himself enjoying it a bit more than he should.

She was attractive, in a down-to-earth sort of way. And he was hard-pressed not to watch her work over him.

"What's your name?" she asked.

His name?

She expected a response, and he meant to give her one. But his brain went dead. And his mind went blank.

Her hands slowed. "You do remember your name, don't you?"

He wondered if his expression looked as dumb-struck as he felt.

Probably so, because she merely stared at him with the damp rag hanging limp in her still hand.

She was waiting for an answer, but he couldn't give her one.

He didn't have any idea who the hell he was.

Chapter Two

*W*here was he?

Louanne had placed the call over an hour ago, and it wasn't like Doc to tarry.

The early afternoon sun poured through the bay window, but that still didn't seem to light the walnut-paneled living room. And even though a gentle breeze filtered through the screen of the open front door, Louanne was reminded of how dark and musty the house had become.

But with finances what they were, she wasn't sure when she'd be able to budget a gallon of paint, let alone a remodel.

She paced the living room floor, feeling as though she was beating down a path in the worn, pea-green carpeting, while waiting for medical reinforcements to arrive.

A small voice suggested that she should have called 9-1-1, that she should have set aside her concerns about anyone knowing she was back in town. But she reminded herself the country doctor had an abundance of experience under his belt. And that he would be able to determine the extent of the man's injuries.

More folks than Louanne could count said that there was no better diagnostician than Dr. Archibald Haines. Of course, they did tend to be the older folks in the community who were resistant to change. But Louanne's parents had also believed it to be true. And she had no reason to doubt the claim.

Aggie and Pete, who were among the chorus of Pebble Creek citizens singing Doc's praises, said they found comfort in seeing the grandfatherly man standing at their sickbed, the worn leather satchel that once belonged to his dad clutched in his capable hands.

Doc was a big man, with a full head of white hair, broad shoulders and a ready smile. A widower in his early eighties, he still stood fairly straight and tall, lived a full life and maintained a small, private practice.

The country physician talked about retirement like it was on the horizon, but he'd become a part of Pebble Creek, and most of the citizens who clung to his counsel and skill wouldn't let him take more than an occasional weekend fishing trip.

The drone of a heavy-duty engine sounded out front, and Louanne hurried to peer out the large picture window that bore dusty smudges from a year or more of neglect. It was Doc, thank goodness. But what was he doing in that brand-new, family-size Winnebago?

It didn't matter, she supposed, just as long as he'd arrived.

She met him on the front porch. "Thanks for coming by."

"Glad I could. I was on my way to Norman, Oklahoma, for the Haines family reunion, and if you would have called me thirty minutes later, I would have been too far along to turn around."

"Then I'm glad I caught you in time." Louanne led him through the small entry and down the hall to the guest room. There, the wounded man lay without his shirt and boots. He still wore his dusty, frayed jeans, but he was cleaner than when she and Pete had found him wandering in a daze.

Those eyes, just as mesmerizing as when she first saw him, snagged her gaze, touching not only her sympathy, but also jogging an awareness of herself as a woman.

The man was just as enigmatic, just as attractive as she remembered. Maybe more so.

Always the romantic and a writer at heart, Louanne imagined him standing on the moors—Heathcliff as Emily Brontë had surely imagined him.

Doc introduced himself, then began a thorough exam. For some reason, Louanne stood in the doorway, unmoving—as though she had every right to hear the diagnosis.

Finally, after probing around the gash near the man's temple, the white-haired country doctor took a seat beside the bed. "What happened to you, son?"

The stranger looked at Doc with those stunning eyes. "I don't know."

"You have any idea what day it is?" the physician asked.

The dark-haired man blew out a sigh, then shook his head.

"You have a name?"

The stranger furrowed his brow, appearing perplexed, then felt for the pockets of his jeans. He reached into the front, right-hand side and withdrew a fold of bills held by a red rubber band.

Unlike men who liked to keep the largest denomination on the outside of a gold money clip to flash impressively, the stranger kept quite a few hundred-dollar bills on the inside, tucked around a silver credit card and a driver's license.

If Louanne had to wager a guess, she would estimate he had close to a thousand dollars on him. Maybe more.

For that reason, she suspected his injuries hadn't been the result of a mugging. Unless he'd come out on top. Still, her gut instinct told her he wasn't a thief.

When he withdrew the driver's license, he studied it momentarily, then glanced at the doctor. "I guess my name is Rowan Parks. And I'm from California."

Doc nodded slowly, then crossed his arms, resting them on an ample belly. "Does that trigger any other recollections?"

The man—Rowan—slowly shook his head. "I'm afraid not. And the motor vehicle mug shot doesn't look familiar, either."

"Well, let's not worry about it just yet. I think, with some rest and quiet, things will come back to you." Doc withdrew a light from his bag, then proceeded to shine it in Rowan's eyes.

"Is he going to be all right?" she asked, realizing she should have kept the question to herself. Or asked the doctor in private.

"I don't see anything worrisome." Doc clicked off the light, took a seat in the chair next to the bed, then turned to Louanne. "He may have a slight concussion, and he'll need a couple of stitches. But the rest of the injuries appear to be minor abrasions and bruises. I've got to go back to the motor home. I've got some supplies that I can't carry in my bag packed away, including what I'll need to flush out that wound."

Louanne followed the white-haired doctor to the door. "What do you think happened to him?"

"Who knows? Car accident, maybe. Or a barroom brawl. He's hurt, but I don't think it's serious. No internal bleeding or broken bones. The biggest concern is the head, but his pupils are responsive, and I don't see any indication of a skull fracture. I think he'll be all right."

Thirty minutes later, after flushing out the wound and washing it with an orangy-brown soap, Doc applied a local anesthetic and carefully placed about five or six stitches to close the gash. Then he took off his rubber gloves and asked Louanne to step outside the guest room.

"What do you think?" she asked.

"He's strong, young and healthy, so I expect him to be back to fighting weight in the next couple of days."

"Do you think he needs to go to the hospital?" she asked.

"Not unless his wound gets infected. But I've got some sample packets of an antibiotic I'll leave with you."

"And what about his memory?" she asked.

"I suspect once he lets his mind rest, things will slowly start making sense to him again. The brain doesn't like getting jostled around like that, so that might account for some confusion."

"And what if his memory doesn't return?" What was she supposed to do with him then?

"Then take him to one of the bigger medical centers in Austin." Doc placed a fatherly hand on her shoulder. "Unless you'd rather get rid of him."

Get rid of him?

It would probably be a smart move. But Louanne—crazy as it may seem—actually welcomed the unexpected interruption to her dull routine, especially since she hadn't left the ranch in nearly a year and a half. "I don't mind if he stays a day or two."

"Good. I'd rather not move him. In fact, I'm going to give him a mild sedative to help him rest."

"And what should I do when he wakes up?" she asked, knowing she had a ton of chores left on her daily list and an infant son to look after.

"Offer him something mild, like broth. And keep him quiet, if you can. Bed rest ought to do wonders."

As Louanne followed Doc to the door, she wondered what she'd gotten herself into.

God knew she no longer craved the drama she and her sister had always wanted in their lives. And she didn't need the additional work or worry.

Still, that wasn't her biggest concern.

For a woman who'd sworn off men for life, the raven-haired hunk had a way of stirring a feminine interest she'd once thought dead.

A curiosity that had once gotten her in a slew of trouble.

The injection Dr. Haines had given the stranger, or rather Rowan, had knocked him out for most of the afternoon, which allowed Louanne to get to some of the household chores she never seemed to have time for.

She washed the windows, mopped the yellowed linoleum in the kitchen and polished the furniture. If anything, her efforts only made her realize how run-down the house had become since her mother's death. Not that it had been a decorator's dream before, but her mother had a way of making the best out of a sorry situation—a trait Louanne was trying hard to acquire as of late.

Maybe that's why her mom had been content—happy, even—with a mason jar full of wildflowers, while Louanne and Lula had wanted crystal vases and long-stemmed red roses.

But those days of youthful discontent were long gone.

Noah's father had seen to that.

A light rap sounded at the screen door, and Louanne looked up from her dusting to see Aggie and Noah on the front porch.

"Hey, there." She set down the bottle of lemon oil and the dirty rag, then wiped her hands on the cotton apron she wore and invited the older woman inside.

Louanne brushed a kiss across Noah's chubby cheek. "Have you been a good boy for Aggie?"

"He's always good for me." The woman, who hadn't been able to have children of her own, adored the baby and never complained. "Of course, he didn't nap very well. I think he's cutting another tooth."

Louanne tugged at her son's little foot and smiled.

"We're going to be feeding you corn on the cob in no time at all."

As Aggie handed the squirmy infant to Louanne, she asked, "How's that fellow doing?"

"He's been sleeping all afternoon, which I think was Doc's intent."

"Mind if I look in on him?" Aggie asked. "You know how Pete is always teasing me about those romance books I read? Well, he said the guy you found looks like one of the cover models."

Rowan Parks was definitely attractive, with a roguish appeal, although Louanne doubted he was a model. But then again, she didn't know who he really was, or what he did for a living. "I put him in Lula's room."

Aggie chuckled. "Bet he thinks he's in Hollywood, with all those old movie posters Lula left on the walls."

"I doubt whether he took much stock in the decor. And, if he did, he didn't say anything."

"Did his memory come back?" Aggie asked.

"Not yet. After Doc left and while he was sleeping, I tried to get his phone number by calling information in the San Francisco area. But it must be unlisted." Louanne blew out a weary sigh. "I'd like to help, to get in touch with his family. They're probably worried about him."

"Why don't you give it a day or so? Maybe he'll be able to remember who he is and call his family himself."

Louanne hoped so. She'd hate to have to contact the sheriff and ask about people reported missing in the area. She suspected Richard had filed a report on her.

Of course, she'd call the sheriff, if she had to. "You're probably right, Aggie. Maybe he'll wake up after a good sleep and remember who he is."

The gray-haired woman grinned. "Then I'd better take that quick peek now."

"Maybe you should." Louanne watched as Aggie tiptoed down the hall and headed toward the room that was available for the guests Louanne would never have, since this old ranch house wasn't the kind of place Lula, or rather Tallulah, would be likely to visit.

It would be nice to see her older sister again, but a trip to California in the near future didn't seem any more likely than a coat of new paint for the inside of the house. Or new carpeting.

And even if Louanne struck black gold or stumbled upon a buried treasure chest in the south pasture, she wasn't going anywhere. Not until she knew Richard Keith was no longer a threat.

As Aggie peered at the sleeping stranger in the guest room, a slow smile tugged at her lips. "Pete was right. That's one good-looking man, even all beat up like that."

Louanne had come to a similar assessment. And she couldn't help wondering what Rowan Parks would look like all decked out for a night on the town.

"Are you sure about him staying here?" the older woman asked. "We don't know anything about him."

Louanne appreciated her friend's concern. But something inside told her the man could be trusted. "I'm sure we'll be just fine."

Aggie pressed a kiss upon Noah's cheek. "You call me and Pete if there's a problem, and we'll come lickety-split."

"I will."

Having Aggie and Pete nearby was truly a comfort, although, on occasion, Louanne still woke in a cold sweat, heart pounding from a nocturnal race to flee the man who threatened to kill her if she ever left him. It had become a familiar nightmare, and one she prayed would never come true.

When Aggie left, Louanne placed Noah in his playpen in the kitchen while she prepared a pot of chicken broth, noodles and vegetables.

There were a ton of things she ought to be doing, but she never had enough quality time to spend with the baby boy who was fast becoming a toddler. And she relished what little time they had together.

Louanne fed Noah his supper, then gave him small chunks of banana to feed himself, while she sat at the table and dined on a bowl of soup.

When her son squished the last few pieces of 'nana into a gooey mess and smeared them across the tray of his secondhand high chair, she cleaned him up then removed him from his cracked, red vinyl seat.

"Time for this little piggy to get ready for bed," she said, as she carried him to the master bathroom.

Noah squealed in delight and anticipation. He loved his bath, just as much as Louanne loved watching him splash and play.

While the old, claw-foot tub filled, Louanne knelt upon the floor and rested her bottom on her feet. She couldn't help her silly grin, as she watched him suck on a wet washcloth.

He smiled back at her, then dropped the cloth and slapped both chubby hands upon the water. A burst of droplets splattered into his face, and he sucked in a breath and blinked.

Louanne laughed, then turned off the spigot. She didn't know how long she sat there, entranced by the child's antics, but before he turned into a shriveled prune, she snatched him from the tub and wrapped him in a towel.

Noah shrieked in protest, until she handed him a rubber ducky to chew on.

Moments later, she had him slicked down with lotion and double diapered for the night. Then she dressed him in the brand-new cowboy jammies that Aggie had bought him for his first birthday.

His powdery, baby scent was a comfort to her, and she brushed a kiss across the downy soft hair on his head. "Sleep tight, little one. Mommy loves you."

He fussed for just a moment, then slipped a thumb into his mouth.

In spite of the regret she felt at having become involved with his father, Louanne loved her son with all her heart. And she counted him as a precious gift and a heavenly blessing.

She whispered a crib-side prayer, before returning to the kitchen to wash the few dishes from their evening meal. She glanced at the pot of homemade chicken noodle soup on the stove.

Should she leave it out for Rowan or put it away?

Before she could decide, the pipes groaned and grumbled through the walls of the hundred-year-old ranch house. Someone—Rowan—had turned on the hot water.

Doc said the man needed bed rest, so she dropped the dish towel on the countertop and hurried down the hall to reprimand her patient.

When she knocked on the bathroom door, he opened it, wearing only a pair of faded jeans with the top button unsnapped. That's how she'd left him, so she shouldn't be taken aback, but he'd been lying down then. Weak and defenseless.

Now he stood more than six feet tall. And when he peered at her through the open door, those angel eyes nearly took her breath away.

"Is something wrong?" he asked.

Yes. No. Corded muscles, a golden brown tan. A sprinkle of dark hair on his chest that trailed down to his belly and beyond.

And she was gawking, for heaven's sake.

But why not? She hadn't seen a man without his shirt in what seemed like ages. And even then, the vision she remembered fell short of the benchmark Rowan Parks set.

"You're supposed to be in bed," she said, "taking it easy and resting."

"I'm dirty. And I don't like the way I smell. So I thought a shower would be a good idea."

"Do you need any help?" The moment she blurted out the question, she wanted to reel it back in, but it was too late. "I mean…can I get you something?"

"I don't suppose you have a razor or a change of clothes?"

Actually, she did. Her father's shaving gear still rested in the master bathroom, and his clothing still hung in the closet.

"I'll get them for you," she said, before padding down the hall.

Moments later, she returned with a washrag and towel, a razor, shaving cream, boxer shorts, an undershirt and a pair of jeans she hoped would fit. When she handed them to him, their hands touched. She pulled away, but not before something warm and magnetic jolted her with sexual awareness.

Had he felt it, too?

She hoped not, but his gaze seemed to linger on her eyes, her face.

"You look familiar," he said.

Her older sister's picture had graced the cover of

People magazine last month. Had he spotted the resemblance she had to Tallulah—minus the makeup
and snazzy clothes, of course? Or was he just trying
hard to recognize someone, something?

It would be sad to have amnesia—if one wasn't
striving for anonymity, like Louanne was.

"I'm sure your memory will return," she said.

They stood rooted in the moment, caught up in
something tangible. Something vibrant and stirring.

And Louanne, who'd felt like a hollow shell for
so long, couldn't seem to ignore the feeling of being
alive again. She was aware of each heady breath she
sucked into her lungs, each zippity-do-da beat of
her heart.

He reached out and gently stroked her cheek with
the back of his knuckles, sending her pulse skidding
throughout her bloodstream.

She didn't pull away, although she should have.
What business did she have fantasizing again?

But as she studied the battered man with hair as
black as a winter night and eyes as blue as the
summer sky, she found it hard not to dream. To
imagine.

Her tongue seemed to wallow in her throat, as she
struggled not to speak, not to reveal her hope that
Rowan would believe she was something more
worldly, more exciting than she really was. She
wanted to cling to the old fantasy, to imagine she
wasn't a woman with sun-dried skin and chapped

hands. To pretend she was once again a graduate student in literature who enjoyed the arts and culture.

"What did you say your name was?" he asked.

It seemed as though his short-term memory had been affected, too, since she'd already told him the country-girl truth.

"You don't remember?" she asked.

Rowan shook his head. No, he *didn't* remember, damn it. Should he?

She'd asked him his name when she first brought him home, as though she didn't know him. But had that been her way of assessing his injury?

Lord, she looked familiar to him. As though he'd known her for years. Was she someone special to him? A wife? A lover?

"My name is Louanne."

It was a Southern name, one that should be enunciated with the charm of a twang or drawl. But she'd shed her accent, if she'd ever had one. And the melodic lilt of her voice lingered on his ears like the sound of a classical harp.

Yet the name didn't mean anything. And for the life of him, he couldn't seem to jump-start the part in his brain that would remind him who she was and what she meant to him.

Tall and lean, she was physically fit, but not from the gym or newfangled diets. The golden-brown tan and solid stance suggested she'd spent long days working in the sun. And she was dressed simply, in denim jeans and a blue plaid blouse. Nothing fancy or alluring.

Yet she had a womanly appeal that drew a man's attention. His appreciation.

Rowan didn't know why he suspected they'd meant something to each other.

The way she looked at him, he supposed. The way he felt drawn to her, her voice. Those golden brown eyes. The attraction they both felt.

The fact she hadn't backed away when he touched her in a familiar way.

What kind of relationship did they have?

He could ask, he supposed. But the fact he hadn't remembered her name seemed to bother her. So he let it ride, hoping the answer would surface—somehow—either in conversation or in the dark and empty abyss of his mind.

"Are you hungry?" she asked. "I have a pot of chicken noodle soup on the stove. It's not as good as my mother used to make, but it's tasty. And it'll fill you up."

"Thank you. I'd like a bowl, if you don't mind." He gripped the doorjamb and nodded toward the shower. "After I clean up."

She nodded, then turned on her heel and padded down the hallway, the long, brown braid swishing down her back, keeping time with the gentle sway of her hips.

A wave of dizziness settled over him, but he didn't

call her back. Instead, he closed his eyes and willed the room to stop spinning.

And when he felt as though his legs wouldn't give out on him, he slipped out of his pants and climbed under the hot, steaming spray.

The old doctor had said not to get his wound wet, but Rowan didn't much care.

For some reason, he didn't think he was a man who adhered to the rules—only those he'd made for himself.

When he climbed from the shower and dried off, he glanced into the steamed-up mirror, then wiped the fog away with the frayed, yellow towel.

The dark-haired, blue-eyed image staring back at him didn't look familiar.

Oh, God. He swore under his breath and willed himself to remember.

Who the hell was he?

His driver's license said he lived in California. But if that were the case, what was he doing in Texas?

He didn't have a clue.

But for some reason, he had a feeling the tall, attractive brunette seemed to hold the answer in the depths of those golden-brown eyes.

Chapter Three

"No!"

Heart pounding, pulse racing, Louanne jerked up in bed and scanned the darkened bedroom lit only by a child's night-light in the hall.

It took a moment for her mind to clear, for her to realize Richard hadn't found her, hadn't slipped into her bedroom to carry out his threat in the dark of night.

"No," the voice cried again. A sleep-graveled male voice. The wounded stranger in Lula's room.

Rowan.

She threw off the covers, slipped out of bed and hurried past the Mother Goose night-light in the hall, pausing in the doorway of the guest room.

Rowan tossed his dark head from one side of the

pillow to the other, but Louanne didn't think he was awake.

Was he caught in the throes of a nightmare? Haunted by memories, as she sometimes was?

Or did the sedative he'd been given continue to linger in his subconscious?

She wasn't sure, but she made her way to his bedside and reached for his arm. "Rowan?"

"Emily," he muttered.

Emily? Was that his wife? Or maybe his lover?

She suspected so. There was no way a man like Rowan was wandering around unattached.

Yet, that's exactly how she'd found him, wandering and lost. Again, his plight tweaked her sympathy. She lifted her hand, placed it softly upon his brow, upon the dark, rebellious locks of his hair. Felt the dampness of his nocturnal struggle for peace.

He was in need of a haircut, she supposed. But the style seemed to suit the vagabond image she held of him. The storyteller inside her soul longed to make sense of his plight, his journey, while the woman in her longed to touch him, to comfort him. To hold him to her breast.

"It's all right," she whispered. "I'm here."

He seemed to settle, or at least the tension in his body eased. He'd shaved this afternoon, but he still bore a rugged, bad-boy aura. Even in sleep.

The romantic in her wanted to wake him, to stir a smile. A heated gaze. Maybe even a kiss.

Foolish woman. Thoughts of romance and candle-light had been her downfall, her Achilles' heel. That and her naïveté, she supposed.

Still, she didn't move away. Didn't retreat back to her room where she belonged. She stayed at his bed-side, uninvited but drawn to him.

She supposed there was no reason for her to sit here, like a motherly woman comforting a lost child. Any vulnerability and helplessness Rowan might have was only momentary and fleeting. A man like him didn't need a woman like her, like who she'd become.

Yet there was something about the devilishly handsome man with the angelic eyes that stirred her soul the way literary works of fiction used to. The way movies on the silver screen had always en-chanted her sister.

Louanne glanced at the posters that still graced the walls of Lula's room. *Gone with the Wind. Roman Holiday. Top Gun. The Breakfast Club.* The ageless classics, as well as those starring the Brat Pack. Lula loved them all.

Now, Tallulah Brown was making her mark on Hollywood. And Louanne was happy for her.

As children, both girls had longed to escape what they'd thought was a boring life. Lula wanted to be-come a movie star, to wear evening gowns and see her name in marquee lights.

And Louanne, too, had dreamed of becoming one of the rich and famous, of being a *New York Times* bestselling author. She'd once hoped to morph into one of the vibrant, worldly characters she'd only read about.

"Hey."

She glanced down at the man in Lula's bed, saw him watching her. Felt his gaze study her. Saw a flicker of masculine interest in his eyes.

"You're awake," she said, her nerve endings alive and responsive. Her hormones soaring.

He nodded. "Yeah. What time is it?"

"I don't know." She glanced at the alarm clock on the scarred oak dresser. "About two o'clock, a little after. I…uh…heard you call out."

"I'm sorry for waking you."

She couldn't actually see the vivid blue of his eyes, but the color was ingrained in her mind. She didn't think she'd ever look at the summer sky again and not think of Rowan Parks. "It's okay. I wanted to check on you anyway. Did you have a nightmare?"

"Yeah." He ran a hand through the tousled, black locks, then grimaced when a finger hit the mended gash on his temple.

"Want to talk about it?"

"Not really. I was running. In the dark."

"You called for someone named Emily," she supplied, hoping it might give his mind a clue to work with.

His brow furrowed, then he shook his head. "I don't know why."

"Maybe she means something to you."

A woman named Emily?

Nothing came to mind, no light in the middle of the darkness.

Rowan shrugged, then sat up in bed. Interestingly enough, the only thing that felt the least bit familiar was the brown-haired woman who sat beside his bed. And she appeared troubled.

Her eyes darted around the room, looking at everything but him.

Why? Did it hurt her to think he'd forgotten about her? About whatever they had together? Or that he'd called out another woman's name?

He was afraid to ask, afraid to try and defend himself or explain without having any knowledge of his past.

She continued to avoid his gaze, so he glanced around the room lit by muted light, saw the old movie posters on the wall. Most of the flicks he'd seen somewhere. Sometime. But he didn't know when or with whom.

"This room used to belong to my sister," Louanne said.

Had he ever met the sister? He didn't have a clue. In fact, the nothingness in his mind was beginning to bother him, more than he cared to admit. And the urge to cling to what felt right, stable and familiar grew steady and strong.

He reached out, took the work-roughened hand

of the woman who cared enough to sit up with him. To worry about him. His thumb made a slow circle on her skin. Her lips parted, as though his touch affected her. As though she felt the same bond he felt.

She gave his hand a faint squeeze. Or was that only his imagination? Wishful thinking, maybe.

For some reason, he found the woman attractive, even wearing a worn, pink flannel gown. She had a simple beauty, a loveliness that drew him to her.

A man would look forward to coming home to a woman like her.

To come home?

Had he felt that way, prior to his injury? Had he been eager to see her?

He tried to tell himself that she was a stranger and no more familiar than this old house. That he'd never met her before. But for some reason, he felt on the verge of recognition each time he looked at her.

But in spite of the familiarity, the feeling of home and hearth, the earthly beauty, he also saw vulnerability in her eyes. Sadness. And he hoped he hadn't been the cause of it.

He wanted to learn more about their relationship, whatever it might be, but didn't want to admit his curiosity. So he skated around the question he really wanted to ask. "Tell me about you, Louanne."

"There's not much to tell."

He had to have met her somewhere. If he was

from California, what was he doing in Texas? Had he chased after her? "Have you always lived here?"

Another wave of sadness darkened her eyes. "I left home after high school and went to college."

Is that where they'd met? He'd gone to college, or at least it felt as though he had. But that's as far as his mind would stretch.

So he asked, "Where'd you go to school?"

"Back east. A small liberal arts college."

Nothing. Back to square one.

But he continued along the same path, the same line of questioning. "What was your major?"

"English."

Still nothing.

"I'm really sorry." And he was. How could he have forgotten her?

"Why are you sorry?" she asked.

"You look so familiar. But I can't remember how we met, what we've been to each other."

Before she could answer, an infant cried out. "Ma. Ma—ma."

A baby? The woman had a child?

Another blank, but this one was more unsettling than the others. How in the hell could Rowan have forgotten something like that?

She must have read curiosity and remorse in his expression. "Excuse me. I have to go see about him."

"Him?"

"Noah. My son."

Her son?

"Is the baby mine?" he asked, unable to hold back the haunting question.

Her mouth parted, but then she recovered. "No, you're not the father."

As Rowan watched her disappear from sight, he wasn't sure whether he was disappointed or not.

As soon as Louanne was sure Noah had fallen back to sleep, she slowly lifted her hand from his small, pajama-clad back and tiptoed from his bedside.

She probably ought to return to Rowan's room and address the awkward question he'd asked her, the question that had come out of the blue and set her imagination soaring.

He'd looked at her as though she'd been an old lover he'd run into unexpectedly.

Is the baby mine?

She'd answered him, of course, but she hadn't taken time to explain to the poor, confused man that they'd just met, that they didn't have a past together. That she and he…well, that they hadn't been involved sexually.

But the fact that he'd so easily assumed they'd once been—or still might be—lovers had flattered her. And, in a way, excited her.

To be honest, she was attracted to the mysterious vagabond who'd wandered into her life. But nothing would become of the growing attraction, because

Louanne wouldn't allow herself to become involved with him—for more reasons than one.

As she started down the hall, she wasn't sure whether she wanted to find Rowan awake or asleep. But the moment she reached his doorway, their eyes met and her pulse quickened.

She placed a hand on the doorjamb, but didn't enter the room; she didn't trust herself to get too close to the gorgeous man lying in bed.

Before she could catch her breath and broach the subject, he slid her a shy, half smile. "You look really familiar to me. And I'm not sure why. But I'm sorry for assuming that we'd…you know."

Yeah. She knew. And, in a way, she was sorry that they hadn't.

She offered what she hoped was a sincere smile. "That's all right. I can't imagine how difficult it must be for you. And I intend to do whatever I can to help you find your past."

Their gazes locked. And for a still, heated moment, his prior assumption and her attraction swirled around them like the first stirring of a Texas twister.

"Well," she said, trying to end the awkward moment. "I'd better get some sleep. I'll see you in the morning."

"Good night."

She went back to her room and climbed into bed, but sleep evaded her until just before the break of dawn, when she gave up hope of a run-in with the sandman and quietly started her day.

About an hour or so later, Noah cried out, and she managed to reach him before he woke Rowan. Then, after changing his diapers, she took her son into the kitchen, where he sat happily in his high chair, drinking milk from his little cup, while she prepared bacon and hotcakes.

The morning sunlight filtered through the age-yellowed lace curtain, dappling the chipped tile countertop. And the aroma of fresh coffee wafted through the house, as the old percolator sputtered and gurgled on the stove, blending with the savory scent of breakfast meat.

A rap sounded at the back door, and Pete let himself in. He took off his hat and hung it on the rack in the service porch, where her daddy used to always leave his. "How'd it go last night?"

"All right," she said, deciding not the mention the nocturnal chat, the caress of her hand. The self-conscious way she'd withdrawn from Rowan's touch as she'd remembered when her skin hadn't been so leathery.

Pete held a purse-like, zippered bag in his hand. "Is he awake?"

"No. Not yet." Louanne cracked an egg into the white ceramic bowl of pancake flour, then tossed the shell into the trash.

"Well, I found out how he got hurt." Pete poured

himself a mug of coffee. "While I was going out to mend that stretch of fence, I found a busted up motorcycle lying in a ditch."

"So he must have crashed."

"Yep. And it was a damn nice bike at that. He was riding one of them fancy Harley-Davidsons. 'Course it don't look so fancy anymore."

It didn't surprise her. Rowan had wealth written all over him, in spite of the worn jeans. "I heard those bikes were expensive."

"At one time," Pete said, "Hells Angels and other biker gangs used to favor those big bikes. But now, they've become popular with those yuppie fellows."

Was Rowan a young professional-type?

The wrecked Harley ought to answer a few questions, like how he'd gotten hurt. But it merely provided more questions about the enigmatic Rowan Parks.

"Anyway, I didn't bring that durn bike back here. It must weigh a ton. But I found this in a saddlebag near the seat." He placed his discovery on the countertop.

Louanne wiped her hands upon the apron, then picked up the leather pouch. Curiosity begged her to unzip it, to look inside. To learn more about the hellion who'd touched something hidden in her soul.

"You gonna open it up?" Pete asked.

A smile teased Louanne's lips. Pete was as curious as an old woman, according to Aggie. And she'd seen his nosy side. "Why don't you tell me what's inside, since you probably already peeked."

He chuckled. "You're as bad as my wife."

Before she could apologize, he said, "I found a California vehicle registration, listing Rowan Parks as the owner. And a few personal items, like breath mints and a checkbook. Plus a cell phone."

Louanne wasn't normally a snoop. Had Rowan been unconscious, she would have had every right to sift through his belongings to notify the next of kin. But he was certainly able to go through his belongings himself. Of course, if the cell phone battery went dead before he got a chance to look at any missed calls, he might never learn who he was. Or be able to alert his friends and family members that he was alive and safe.

"You want me to take this little feller to Aggie?" Pete asked, as he poked a callused finger at Noah's belly and received a squeal and a smile for his efforts.

"Sure. But he hasn't had his breakfast yet."

"Aggie loves feeding him."

"I know." Louanne smiled warmly and gave the man a hug. "In case you've forgotten, I appreciate how much you and Aggie do for us. And how much you love Noah."

"We love you, too, honey. You've been like the daughter we never had." Pete removed the happy child from the high chair. "Come on, li'l pardner. Let's go say hello to Aggie."

When Louanne was alone in the kitchen, she picked up Rowan's cell phone. It looked like a top-of-the-line model. Fancy and expensive, like his Harley. Like his Rolex. It suited him, she supposed. Or at least the picture of him she was forming.

As soon as she'd figured out how the bells and whistles worked, she pulled up a list of phone numbers. The one on top belonged to "Sam." She jotted down the number, just in case the battery died.

"What are you doing?"

Louanne jumped at the sound of the masculine voice, turning to see Rowan standing in the kitchen doorway, looking like a sleep-tousled dream-come-true.

She held up his cell phone. "Good news—I think. Pete found a wrecked Harley-Davidson not far from where we found you. This leather pouch and a cell phone were in the saddlebag. You've programmed numbers in here, so we have a way of accessing your past."

He just leaned against the doorjamb, unsmiling.

She would have thought he'd be eager to find out who his friends and family were. Who Emily was. "What's the matter?"

"I don't know." He raked a hand through the tumble of dark, rebellious locks, not making the strands look any better or worse. "Maybe it's the dream I had last night."

She didn't doubt he'd found it disturbing. "What about the dream?"

"I was running from something."

Like she was running and hiding? "From whom?"

"No one in particular. It was more of a force, a presence. From feelings like grief and anger." He shrugged. "It's hard to explain, but I don't feel a pressing need to go home, wherever that is."

"Maybe it's the amnesia that has you uneasy."

Not knowing who he was and how he fit into the scheme of life had to be confusing and unsettling, to say the least. And she suspected it could cause a person to become a bit paranoid.

How would she feel if her memory suddenly vanished? If those frightening images of Richard no longer surfaced, no longer haunted her days and nights?

She might sleep better, but would her fear remain as a faceless, unidentifiable threat?

"Maybe you're right." Rowan took a deep breath, then blew out a ragged sigh. "The amnesia—not being able to remember who I am—has left me a bit unbalanced."

"Aren't you curious about the past, the people in your life?"

"Yeah. But I can't explain the discontent, the uneasiness I feel."

"People might be worried about you."

"And they might not give a rat's hind end about me." He raked a hand through his hair again. "See what I mean? I keep getting these weird feelings, and I don't know where in the hell they come from."

"Calling up your past can wait," she said, understanding, at least to some extent, his reluctance. "If that's what you want."

"That's the problem. I don't know what I want. Or what those people mean to me." He nodded toward the cell phone she held, then shoved his hands into the front pockets of his jeans. He looked so tough, so vulnerable.

"The call can wait. You can make it whenever you're ready."

"Thanks." His heavenly eyes lingered on hers and revealed sincerity and appreciation. But that wasn't all. When he looked at her, the room seemed to come alive with sexual awareness, something she didn't want to consider and didn't dare question or pursue.

Several hours later, while Noah was napping at Aggie's and Louanne was hanging a batch of wet sheets on the clothesline, Rowan joined her outside.

The afternoon sun glistened on the black strands of his hair, like a kiss of sunlight on a raven's wing in flight. And she found it difficult not to stare. Not to let romantic notions kidnap her thoughts and ride off in the sunset.

"Maybe it would be a good idea if you made that call," he said. "But keep things generic and brief. You can say I need some time to myself. Then you can gauge their reactions."

"All right. I'm nearly done here." She hung the last sheet on the line, but before she could pick up the empty wicker laundry basket, he snatched the handle at one end and carried it into the house. She followed behind, watching the swagger of his walk, the way he filled out her father's shirt and jeans in a way the tall, lanky, older man never had.

Once inside, Louanne glanced at the phone number she'd written on the notepad by the phone. "The first one belongs to someone named Sam. Does that name sound familiar?"

"No."

She picked up the receiver of the wall-mounted kitchen phone and dialed. A moment later, a recorded message answered.

That was odd. She looked at Rowan, caught his gaze. "The number is no longer in service, and there's no new number. How up-to-date is your phone list?"

"You're asking me?" Rowan rolled his eyes and blew out a ragged sigh.

"Sorry." She picked up the cell phone and glanced at the display. The second entry was a bit disturbing. "I brought this up last night, but I'd better ask again. Does the name Emily ring a bell?"

"No. It still doesn't."

Well, nevertheless, there *was* a woman in his life named Emily, a woman he'd called for last night in his dream. And for some reason, that fact was a little unsettling.

But she brushed her discomfort aside. No doubt

Emily missed her man. Louanne certainly would, if her husband or lover turned up missing.

She picked up the kitchen phone and gave it another shot. After four rings, an answering machine kicked on, and a female voice said, "You've reached 555-4349. There's no one to take your call right now, but if you leave your name and number after the tone, we'll get back to you."

We'll get back to you?

Was that a single woman's ploy to make it appear she didn't live alone? Or were Emily and Rowan live-in lovers? Or maybe even married?

Last night, Rowan had looked at Louanne and touched her in such a loving, gentle way—the way a man touched a woman he wanted sexually. Not that Louanne was an expert at that sort of thing, but she knew the look, the touch.

She'd pulled away, of course, for a variety of reasons that had nothing to do with the way his fingertips had sent a shimmy of heat pulsing through her veins.

Now she was even more glad that she hadn't let things go any further. What if she would've let their attraction build?

Rowan might be spoken for—by a woman named Emily. A woman whose recorded voice sounded young, nice and pretty— if a person could gather that kind of information from an answering machine.

At the beep, Louanne left her name and number,

mentioning Rowan and asking Emily to call her back. Then she hung up.

The third entry in line was someone named Brenda. Another woman? Was Rowan playing the field?

She glanced at him. "How about Brenda?"

He shrugged. "Why don't I go take another shower? I'm not used to the Texas humidity. Besides, I don't feel up to an awkward conversation with people I can't remember."

When he left her alone in the kitchen, she gave it one more try—just for the heck of it. And this time, her call was rewarded.

"Parks residence. May I help you?"

For a moment, her tongue deserted her. She'd been halfway prepared to talk to Sam or Emily, but they hadn't answered. This time someone had.

Louanne was well aware of the fact that Rowan had a past, a history. People in his life. But those people were strangers to her—to both of them, right now.

Did Rowan have a loving home? A shady past? Friends and family who cared about him?

Or demons to outrun, like Louanne did.

Suddenly, she understood his apprehension, his fear. At least to some extent. She took a breath and forced herself to speak. "My name is Louanne Brown, and Rowan Parks asked me to call."

"You're calling for Rowan?" The woman's voice wobbled. "Where is he?"

"In Texas."

"But is he all right?"

"He wrecked his motorcycle and received a few bumps, bruises and cuts in the process. But a doctor looked him over and said that he was fine."

"Oh, dear God," the woman said, before blurting out a loud, drawn-out "Emily! Come quick."

A sob sounded on the other end of the line, and Louanne suspected the woman who'd answered had broken down and cried.

Moments later, another female voice came on the line. "This is Emily Parks. What seems to be the problem?"

Emily *Parks?* The lump that had formed in Louanne's throat merely grew larger, and she found it nearly impossible to speak, to respond. To think.

Was he…were they…married? It would seem so. But it really didn't matter. Louanne and Rowan were merely strangers, ships passing in the night.

But if that was the case, why did she feel as though someone had let the wind out of her sails and left her adrift on a lonely sea?

Chapter Four

Louanne gripped the receiver until her knuckles whitened, as she tried to gather her thoughts, her words. "Rowan asked me to call and let you know that he's safe."

"Thank goodness. Where is he?"

"On my ranch in Texas."

Emily paused momentarily, probably trying to make sense of it all. "Who is this?"

"My name is Louanne Brown."

"I appreciate your call," Emily said. "Rowan stormed out of here like a bat out of hell the other night, and I was afraid he'd have an accident. Then a man from the police department called about an hour ago and reported that they'd found his motorcycle in a ditch in Texas. Needless to say, we've been worried."

It sounded as though Rowan had left in anger. Isn't that what Emily had meant by saying he'd stormed out of the house?

Louanne looked to the empty doorway, wishing that Rowan were standing there, so that he could advise her on what or how much to say. But what good would that have done? Rowan couldn't even remember Emily, let alone leaving home like that.

It was hard to second-guess what had happened, but maybe Rowan had a good reason for the grief and anger that had haunted his dream last night.

Had Emily upset him? Caused him to end their relationship? Maybe she'd been the one to put the kibosh on things.

Had Rowan wanted to forget something? Had his amnesia been a bit self-serving?

Louanne had always enjoyed her psych classes in college, but she really wasn't qualified to analyze what was going on in Rowan's relationships, even if she couldn't help herself from doing so.

Besides, speculating wouldn't do any good at this point.

"Was Rowan hurt in the accident?" Emily asked.

"Five stitches was the worst of it." Louanne ignored the amnesia that still plagued him. "But he'll be all right. He just wanted me to call so you wouldn't worry."

"Thank you," Emily said. "Can I please speak to my brother?"

Her brother? Emily was Rowan's sister? For some reason Louanne refused to dwell upon, she felt a sense of relief. "He's not available right now, but I can have him call you back?"

"Did he tell you about the…blowup?" Emily asked.

"He vented a little bit," Louanne lied, wondering if that would free Rowan's sister to reveal any of the details. "I figure there's always two sides to every story."

"Rowan was furious with our father, but that, of course, was nothing new. His anger has been steadily brewing for years." Emily blew out a heavy sigh. "Rowan's probably better off with you in Texas, at least until he cools off. They've never seen eye to eye. And quite frankly, I'm worried one of them will do or say something foolish, something that can't be undone or forgotten."

"I understand," Louanne said, although she didn't. Still, she was glad she'd made the call, that she'd been able to ease the minds of those in the Parks family, of Emily in particular. "I left a message at your house with my number, but if you have a pen and paper, I'll give it to you again."

The muffled sound of a drawer opening and closing came over the line. "Go ahead."

After Louanne recited her telephone number, Emily said, "Thanks again for the call. And for looking out for my brother. I appreciate it."

"You're welcome." Louanne tried to dig for a bit more information. "By the way, who is Brenda?"

"Brenda Wheeler is my father's housekeeper. She more or less raised us, after my mother…left home. So, when she learned about the accident, she was beside herself."

"And Sam?" Louanne asked.

"I don't know anyone by that name. Why do you ask?"

"No reason." Louanne twirled the phone cord around her finger. "Rowan mentioned something about him, that's all. And I was curious, but hated to pry."

"Well, I can understand that. My brother isn't one to open up to anyone, especially his family. So, you'll have to ask Rowan about the man."

"I will," Louanne said, realizing she'd learned very little to help trigger the return of Rowan's memories.

"Listen," Emily added, "If Rowan feels like discussing what happened the other night, have him give me a call at home. I'm not sure it's a good idea to call back here until our father settles down. He's used to having things go his way and can be pretty unreasonable sometimes."

"I'll give Rowan the message," Louanne said, before ending the call.

After the line disconnected, Emily hung up the telephone receiver in the library, the same room in which Rowan had locked horns—*again*—with their father, just two weeks ago. The night their father had accused Rowan of being a family traitor, of revealing secrets and discussing old gossip with strangers.

Knowing Rowan, the accusation couldn't have been any further from the truth. But then, Walter Parks didn't particularly like or trust his youngest son, let alone *know* him.

Emily had always tried hard to keep peace between her siblings and the patriarch, but it was getting more and more difficult to do so.

It was odd that Rowan hadn't placed the call himself, but he'd always been private and evasive. Besides, she suspected that he'd wanted to avoid the risk of having to talk to their father, if he would have answered the phone.

And it was just as well that he hadn't called. Their father was a difficult man, one who didn't find much value in reaching a compromise—with anyone.

Walter Parks had commandeered a jewelry business into an empire over the past thirty years, but he'd never been a loving father, unless one counted providing a silver-spoon existence.

All things considered, growing up had been tough on each of the four Parks children. They'd been abandoned by their mother—intentionally or not—and neglected by their father. But things had been even more difficult for Rowan, whose rebellious nature had always riled the patriarch in one way or another.

Maybe her little brother would find the peace he'd always wanted in Texas.

"Rowan's all right?" Brenda asked, clearly concerned about the man she'd raised.

"He's safe and sound." Emily gave the loving, gray-haired housekeeper a hug goodbye. "I've got to go, Brenda. I'll see you later." Then she grabbed her purse from the sofa.

On the way to the front door, she passed her father's home office, where Linda Mailer was digging through a box of files. The accountant's shoulder-length red hair hid her face like a veil.

Linda looked up and caught her breath. "You startled me."

Why? What had Linda been searching for? Something that didn't concern her?

Oh, for goodness sake. Was Walter's growing paranoia contagious and snaking its way into the minds of the entire family?

The shy, thirty-year-old CPA was a bit young for the trusted position, but she was bright, efficient and devoted to her boss—something a man like Walter Parks undoubtedly appreciated.

Emily shook off the crazy suspicion. "I'm sorry, Linda. I didn't mean to sneak up on you. I was just leaving."

"That's all right. I was so engrossed and caught up in my own world, that I didn't expect to see anyone."

"Well, I'll let you get back to your work." Emily gave a partial wave. "Goodbye."

Linda, with her hands still on the files she'd been perusing, continued her search. She didn't usually work out of the home office, but today she was reconciling Walter's personal accounts and needed to gather some information he kept at the house. And so far, she'd only uncovered a handful of what was needed.

She wasn't sure why she was digging through this box. Curiosity, she supposed. Earlier, Walter had been searching for something in here. He'd run his fingers though his hair and mumbled to himself. Appearing agitated and distressed, he'd suddenly grabbed a file from this box and left the room, which hadn't seemed to relieve his anxiety.

Walter kept a safe in his den, so Linda assumed that's where he'd been going. But he hadn't come back. And about fifteen minutes later, she'd heard his car start up and drive away.

Over the course of an hour, her curiosity had grown. And the old file box had steadily drawn her attention. As she flipped through the contents, not looking for anything in particular, she spotted a yellowed paper—a memo of some kind—resting between two unrelated files. She withdrew the page, intent on filing it properly, but scanned it first so she could determine where it belonged.

She furrowed her brow. That was strange. It was

written twenty-five years ago and mentioned raw diamonds and a cargo drop-off location.

It also bore a name that sounded familiar. *Van Damon.* Wasn't that also the name of the infamous Dutch warlord in Africa?

What a weird coincidence. Walter Parks couldn't possibly be involved in gem smuggling.

Of course, the media had been coming down hard on him, lately. And there were rumors—although Linda didn't believe them.

But as she placed the paper in her briefcase with the intention of taking it back to the main office, something niggled at her.

Back in Texas, Rowan walked into the living room, refreshed from his shower. Through the open screen door, he spotted Louanne standing on the porch and gazing into the horizon.

"Did you get hold of anyone?" he asked.

She turned slowly and rested against the wooden railing. "You and your father had a falling out a couple of nights ago, and it wasn't the first time. For some reason, you charged out of the house in California. And you ended up in Texas."

A falling out with his father? Maybe that's where his sense of anger came from. But what about the grief? Had he been sorry about leaving? Sorry about the rift?

The revelation of his flight to Texas only brought

on more questions. "Do you know what we fought about?"

Louanne shrugged. "I don't know, but it sounds as though you and your dad haven't gotten along for years."

Assuming her suspicion was right, Rowan couldn't help wondering why. But, since the answer was nowhere to be found, he let that question drop and asked another. "Did you find out who Emily is?"

"She's your sister. And she was worried about you. It was a good thing we called, because she'd just received word that your motorcycle was found in a ditch, and no one had any idea what had happened to you."

Maybe Rowan shouldn't work so hard at trying to remember. He'd gotten mad and taken off with the intention of putting a lot of crap behind him. So why not let well enough alone?

Because not being able to remember, to understand, put him at a disadvantage. So, hoping to unleash a flood of memories—or maybe just a trickle—he asked, "Did you find out who Sam is?"

Rowan assumed the man listed at the top of his telephone list had the number one spot for a reason.

"Your sister doesn't know a man named Sam. Could it be a woman? Maybe a nickname for Samantha?"

"You're asking me?"

She slid him a crooked smile, one that made a single dimple in her cheek. "Sorry."

Yeah. He was sorry too. The dark hole that used to be his memory was still just as large, just as empty.

He studied the tall, willowy woman who'd taken him in. The familiar face that drew him to her, those golden-brown eyes that tugged at him. There was a sadness about her, and he wasn't sure why.

"And what about you," Rowan asked. "Where is your family?"

She seemed to ponder his question, and for a moment, he wondered whether she'd answer. "There's not much to tell. For the most part, it's just Noah and me. My parents died in a small plane crash on their way to a cattle auction last year."

"I'm sorry."

"Me, too. More so now that I don't have a chance to tell them how much I loved them, how much I appreciated what they'd provided for my sister and me."

A frown marred her brow, and he had the urge to console her. To step close and take her in his arms. Breathe in her earthy, flowery scent.

He jammed his hands in the front pockets of his jeans instead.

She appeared to be a strong woman. Independent. And not afraid of hard work.

Too much work, he suspected. Did she get any help on the ranch, other than what the old man named Pete could provide?

"Where's your sister?" he asked.

"She's in Australia right now, shooting a movie."

"Your sister is an actress?" He couldn't keep the surprise from his voice, his expression.

Louanne smiled, this one kind of wistful, but revealing a matching set of dimples. "It was always a dream of hers. And I'm proud of her. She made that dream come true."

Would he recognize the name of the actress? He hadn't seen many movies lately.

He hadn't seen many movies lately.

Rowan blinked, sobering as he realized he'd just dug up something from his past—albeit nothing important. But it was a start.

"What's your sister's name?"

"Tallulah Brown."

The tall, glamorous brunette with bronze skin and a body made for a skimpy bikini had starred in the newest James Bond flick.

A smile tugged at the corner of his mouth. He knew who the shapely actress was. And he began to wonder if that's what he'd recognized in Louanne. A resemblance to her movie-star sister.

"You look like her." He realized that was another thing his mind had processed without revealing something he might actually find useful.

"Thanks. I guess." Louanne chuckled. "I'm afraid Tallulah's far more eye-catching and memorable than I am."

Maybe so, but Louanne had a wholesome beauty that didn't need makeup or fancy clothes. And his gut instinct suggested she would look pretty damn good in a bikini, too.

He wondered whether she chose to wear worn, bleached-out jeans and plain, button-down shirts because she couldn't afford anything different, anything new. He scanned the porch of the run-down ranch house. Chipped white paint. A bent window screen. A warped front door. Most things needed to be repaired, refurbished or replaced.

Money was tight, he suspected. And it had been for a very long time. The upkeep on this place had to be an uphill battle, one the single mother appeared to be losing.

Tallulah Brown, on the other hand, had to be doing pretty well. "Doesn't your sister help with any of the expenses?"

Louanne tightened her grip on the wooden porch railing, then released as a splinter poked at her palm.

"What's the matter?" he asked, clearly unaware of how his question had prickled her, how it had triggered thoughts of the past. Thoughts of the secret she kept.

He waited for an answer, but she didn't know how much to tell, how much to reveal. She'd been keeping quiet, protecting her identity as well as her secret for so long, that she felt awkward talking about something that was simple. Easy to understand, at least for her.

It probably seemed reasonable, to an outsider, that the girls share in the ever-constant monthly expenses, both expected and not.

"I can't ask for my sister's help. Or rather, I won't."

"Why not?"

Pride, she supposed, although it went much deeper than that. "When my parents died, Lula begged me to sell the Lazy B. She couldn't see pouring money into a hundred acres that, over the years, wrung out every dream our parents ever had, along with each drop of their blood, sweat and tears."

"And you refused to sell?"

He probably suspected she held an emotional attachment to the time-battered house, to her parents' memories. But that wasn't the case. Louanne had actually agreed with her sister about putting it on the market. Lord knew they needed the money.

Last spring she and Pete had sold off half the cattle to pay the taxes and make ends meet. Several times, their neighbor to the east, Jim Simmons, had offered to buy the property and the remaining cattle, but Louanne desperately needed a place to hide, a place to bear and raise her baby where Richard would never find her. And since she'd followed Lula's lead and created a more cosmopolitan past than growing up on a small, struggling cattle ranch, she felt relatively safe here.

And not in Austin, where he was likely to focus his search.

"Yes, I refused to sell."

"Because of the memories?"

"Yes," she said, the lie resting in the midst of the truth. "I came home because of the memories."

But not the ones he imagined. She returned because of the black, heart-pounding ones provoked by Dr. Richard Keith, the father of her baby. And because of a haunting threat he'd made. A threat that held enough promise to make her flee from college just months before she could finish her graduate work in English.

I'll see you back in my bed...or in a casket, six feet underground.

Louanne had covered her tracks and returned home, where the Lazy B provided refuge and safety for herself and her son—unless Richard took time to unravel her lies and carefully laid plans.

"It looks as though you could use a little financial help." Rowan perused the old house and the yard.

"We're okay. Noah and I don't need anything fancy." *Just a roof over our heads, warm beds to sleep in and enough food to eat.*

"Fancy isn't what I meant." Rowan scanned the outside of the weathered, clapboard house. "Maybe your sister would contribute to a new paint job."

"I don't need her help." Okay, so that wasn't true, but Louanne didn't have the nerve to ask for a loan or for any financial assistance from Lula, particularly when her sister had been so adamant about selling the place.

Life wasn't easy. But it was safe.

She crossed her arms, hoping Rowan would sense how stubborn she could be when necessary. But before he could respond, Noah cried out from his crib, alerting Louanne that he wanted his mommy and her comfort.

Relief settled around her. She was more than ready to escape the questions, the reminders. More than ready to put the memory behind her for a while. Rowan seemed as interested in digging up her past as he was in uncovering his own.

And Louanne was determined to keep her tracks covered and her secret safe.

Later that afternoon, after Aggie had taken Noah for a walk, Louanne put on a ham hock and a pot of beans to cook. She'd become pretty adept at creating nourishing and tasty dishes that didn't cost very much to prepare.

While dinner simmered on the stove, she reached into the cupboard, where her mom and dad used to hide the candy treats they kept for special occasions. She'd continued the practice for Noah, even though he wasn't old enough to eat hard candy.

She popped a lemon drop into her mouth, savored the tart, citrusy taste and suspected an ulterior motive. Maybe the treats were for herself, so she could enjoy a sweet memory every now and again.

After setting the dining room table, she wandered into the living room, where Rowan had stretched out on the tweed sofa that had been in the same spot for as long as she could remember. Her dad used to nap there, too, on Sunday afternoons. After the church service and a hearty dinner with his wife and daughters.

It was a bit odd to have a man in the house again, even though Rowan's stay would be brief. But it was kind of nice, too. She liked the way her heart beat a bit faster whenever she looked at him, whenever he looked at her. Maybe because it made her feel alive again.

When she'd given up graduate school and come home, she was thankful to find refuge. But she also struggled with the realization that she'd come home to wither and die.

It helped that she no longer lost herself in a fictional world behind the covers of a book, or that she no longer worked on the next great American novel. Exercising her imagination would only make her sorry life more miserable. Make her long for something she couldn't allow herself to have.

Louanne eased closer to the sofa, drawn to the man who was still very much a stranger. Yet for some reason, she felt the need to protect him, to help him heal in body and spirit.

She studied Rowan as he slept. A lock of black hair flopped onto his forehead, and his lips parted in slumber. Her eyes traced the faint white line of the old scar that cut into his eyebrow, as well as the new gash Doc had stitched. But neither imperfection was enough to hamper his looks.

He was a handsome man, almost pretty. And she wondered whether he wore his hair unkempt to harden his appearance.

Devil or angel?

Maybe a little of both.

His wound seemed to be mending. There wasn't any sign of swelling or redness. She had a feeling Doc would call to check on his patient. He always did.

While she stooped to check Rowan's stitches, he moved. And she froze, not wanting to disturb him. Not wanting him to see her fuss over him.

Rowan woke to the scent of wildflowers, and when he opened his eyes, he saw Louanne standing over him. Her gaze locked on his, and she chewed her bottom lip. Feeling guilty for being so close?

"I...uh." Her lips parted, and her sweet, lemon-tinged breath nearly made him sit up and beg for a taste. "I thought I'd look at those sutures and make sure they're all right. I don't think you were supposed to get them wet."

"Go ahead and check them," he said, liking the way she hovered over him. The way she wrinkled her brow. The way that golden-brown gaze clung to his.

She didn't move away. And she didn't appear overly interested in his wound. She remained close enough to touch, caught up in something, just like he was.

He wanted to kiss her, to hold her. To feel something other than the nothingness that held him captive. His hand seemed to have a mind of its own, as it slipped under the single braid she wore, finding the back of her neck and drawing her lips to his.

It wouldn't have surprised him in the least if she would've pulled way. Objected. Given him hell for being so forward. But there didn't seem to be anything he could do to avoid the overwhelming urge to taste her.

When his lips brushed her mouth, she didn't fight. Didn't protest. Didn't stiffen.

He took pleasure in the softness that promised to envelop him and relished the intoxicating scent of wildflowers in a green meadow.

Her lips parted, allowing him entrance, and he savored the sweet, lemon-drop taste.

As his tongue sought hers, a jolt of heat jumpstarted his pulse, causing his blood to race, to pound. She must have felt it, too, because she whimpered in response, and her fingers snaked into his hair.

He wanted to draw her body to his, to pull her on top of him. To press her hips against him. And he would have, if the baby hadn't shrieked. And footsteps and a "yoo-hoo" hadn't sounded from the front porch.

Her breath caught, and she slowly pulled away, breaking the kiss. Her hand slipped from his jaw.

But she couldn't hide the desire blazing in those golden eyes. Couldn't hide the effect he'd had on her.

And he knew in that moment, that he would kiss her again and again.

Longer. And deeper.

If he ever got another chance.

Chapter Five

Louanne didn't know what had gotten in to her. She had no business kissing Rowan. In fact, she had no business kissing anyone. Not now, maybe not ever.

And she'd been caught red-handed, or rather red-faced. What would Aggie say?

"We're home," the older woman called from the screen door. "And you'll never guess what we saw."

The warmth in Louanne's cheeks suddenly blazed, her embarrassment flashing like a fire truck on its way to a three-alarm fire.

What had Aggie seen?

An aura of guilt hovered over her, as she faced the consequences of the thoughtless urge to kiss the man with more than his fair share of pheromones.

She should have balked, should have pulled away when Rowan drew her mouth to his. But when his the-sky-is-the-limit gaze promised a toe-curling encounter, a slow and steady flame began to warm her blood and thaw her heart. For a moment, she felt a stir in the imaginative spirit she'd thought had died behind the ivy-covered walls of Cedar Glen College.

And for that reason, she hadn't given the bay window or the open front door a second thought.

Get a grip, she told herself. It was bad enough that she'd lost her head and kissed Rowan like there was no tomorrow—or rather, like there'd been no yesterday, no impeccably-dressed college professor who'd morphed into a monster. No threat that still lingered in her ears. No reason to stay hidden and locked away from the world.

Would Aggie assume Louanne wanted to jump the bones of the first man she'd come into contact with in a year and a half? That's probably what the kiss looked like, especially since Rowan was a stranger. Even to himself.

Louanne drew on what little acting skill Lula had taught her while growing up, and tried to pretend nothing had happened.

Rowan *hadn't* kissed her. And Aggie *hadn't* arrived to witness it.

"Hey, Pumpkin." Louanne opened the front door, brushed a kiss across her son's chubby cheek and smiled brightly. "Did you have a good time?"

"Mah!" Noah smiled, revealing four front teeth and dribbling a tiny drop of drool to his chin.

"Tell Mama what we saw," Aggie prompted.

Louanne's heart burst into her throat, and she tried to come up with some kind of excuse, an explanation for what Aggie had witnessed, since it didn't appear as though a denial would work.

Noah lurched in excitement. "Duh."

"Duckies," Aggie interpreted. "We saw a whole passel of them swimming in the fishing hole."

Oh, thank goodness. Louanne felt Rowan's eyes on her back, even though she couldn't see them. What had he been thinking? That they'd been caught? That they shouldn't have kissed in the first place? That it had been too hot and too good not to kiss one more time?

Noah reached out his pudgy little hands, and Louanne swept him into her arms, glad to have something to hold on to. Something to shield her from the realization that she was still a red-blooded woman with sexual needs.

"Thanks for taking him on your walk, Aggie. The simplest things are such a thrill for him."

"For me, too," the older woman said, as she scanned the living room and spotted Rowan. "Oh, hello there."

Thank goodness. Aggie hadn't seen anything, nor had she picked up any vibes about a kiss that shouldn't have taken place. And apparently her dear friend wasn't aware of the desire that ricocheted throughout the living room.

Louanne softly blew out the breath she'd been holding. "Aggie, this is Rowan Parks."

The plump, gray-haired woman stuck out her hand, then smiled sheepishly. "I took a little peek at you yesterday. While you were sleeping. But it's nice to meet you. In person, I mean."

"Same here." Rowan stood, accepted the customary greeting and smiled. He didn't appear to be ruffled or flustered, not even on the inside, like Louanne was.

"Well," Aggie said, clapping her hands together. "Looks like we've got a foursome for cards. Are you guys interested in a game tonight?"

Louanne figured Aggie was hoping to get to know Rowan better, to size him up.

After all, just last week, the older woman had invited Louanne to attend the marathon bingo tournament at St. Mark's Church. "You need to make friends," Aggie had explained.

"You're my friend," Louanne had countered.

"I mean friends your own age. Besides, you'll never find a man if you don't leave the ranch. And there are a lot of women with unmarried sons and nephews who are dying to see them with a nice girl who'd make a good wife. And they won't give a hoot about you having a baby."

Having a child out of wedlock and the resulting small-town community whispers had been Louanne's reason for asking Pete and Aggie to keep her return and Noah's birth a secret. And as far as Louanne knew, no one in Pebble Creek—other than Doc and their quiet-spoken neighbor, Jim Simmons—knew she was back in town with a baby. Doc had promised not to tell, and Jim, who lived alone, hardly spoke more than ten words a year—and those had to be pried out of him.

"This is a new century," Aggie had added. "Unwed mothers aren't looked down upon like they once were."

When Louanne had told the well-intentioned woman that she didn't like crowds, that she preferred staying home, Aggie must have assumed Louanne suffered from a case of agoraphobia, because she'd said, "Why don't you call Doc Haines and tell him how you feel? I hear they've got medicine for that now."

Rather than go into detail, Louanne had decided to let the assumption of an anxiety disorder stand— unchallenged.

"So what do you say?" Aggie asked, drawing Louanne back to the present. "Playing cards will be fun."

Louanne glanced at Rowan and tried to gauge his reaction to the suggestion.

"I don't mind," he said. "Louanne?"

She smiled, first at Rowan, then at her friend. "All right. I'll put Noah down about 7:00. Why don't you and Pete come over after that?"

"Good. And I'll bring some goodies to eat."

No one made goodies like Aggie. She always had a couple of treats to choose from—cookies, brownies, a lemon meringue pie. It was a wonder Pete stayed so lean, especially when his wife hadn't.

"I'll put on a pot of coffee," Louanne said, as she walked her friend to the door. Under normal circumstances, she might've thought having company tonight would make things awkward, especially since Pete and Aggie had become such close friends and were so protective of her and Noah. But since having someone else in the house this evening might actually defuse whatever was going on between her and the stranger who'd turned her senses on edge, she felt a vague sense of relief.

After that kiss they'd shared, Louanne wasn't sure she wanted to deal with the inevitable question that would follow.

Now what?

But when Aggie went home, Louanne was left to face Rowan. There was no point in averting her gaze and avoiding the subject. Because, try as she might, she couldn't ignore his presence.

Their eyes met, and the kiss stretched between them, connecting them long after it had ended and binding them in a way she wasn't ready for. In a way she might never be ready for.

What should she do? Ignore the fact that it had happened? Broach the subject, getting it over with? Then put it to bed?

Oops. Wrong choice of words.

Maybe she ought to let Rowan bring up the touchy subject.

But when he didn't mention a word, she wasn't sure whether she should be relieved or disappointed.

Rowan stood on the front porch and watched the sun sink low in the West Texas sky. He'd found it a bit weird that Louanne had never mentioned the kiss. He could have done so, he supposed, but he hadn't.

He'd never been one to analyze a sexual relationship; it either worked or it didn't.

He didn't analyze sexual relationships.

Another revelation. Was his memory going to come back one little piece at a time?

The screen door squeaked open, and Louanne joined him on the porch, the baby boy riding on her hip. The little tyke was kind of cute, even though he didn't have much hair. But his eyes were the same golden-brown hue as his mother's, and just as captivating.

"Can you watch Noah while I put dinner on the table?" she asked.

Him? Baby-sit? Rowan hated to tell Louanne no, not after she'd been so good to him. But what the hell did he know about babies or small kids?

He didn't know anything about infants or children.

Great. He'd just remembered another piece of information, which didn't seem particularly useful. He didn't have kids and felt awkward around them.

"Maybe I should set the table instead," he said, hoping for a reprieve. What if he dropped the little guy?

"You're not afraid of a baby, are you?" Her rich, whiskey-hued eyes held a taunt, a tease. A challenge.

"Afraid? No. But I've got to admit, the idea of taking care of one makes me uneasy."

"You don't have to hold him," Louanne said, "if you're not comfortable doing that. But can you make sure he doesn't climb onto the sofa and fall down? Make sure he doesn't eat a handful of potting soil or munch on one of the leaves of the houseplant on the table?"

"Yeah, I can probably handle that." He reached out, and surprisingly, the baby went right to him.

The kid felt kind of weird in his arms. Not heavy, but solid and warm. A little wiggly. His diaper-clad butt was thick and pudgy. Thank goodness she hadn't asked him to change his pants. Rowan wouldn't do that—ever. What a nasty job.

He looked at the baby boy and found the little guy watching him intently. "What's up, kid?"

Noah grinned, then pointed toward the horizon and grunted.

"You want to go for a walk?"

The kid lurched in his arms, indicating Rowan had understood what "umphd" meant.

"Okay, but we're not going far. I have to stay close to your mom. Just in case we both got more than we bargained for in this baby-sitting arrangement."

The baby grinned from ear to ear as though he thought they'd struck a hell of a deal.

A couple moments later, as Rowan stood under a sycamore tree and Noah reached for a leaf, Louanne called them to dinner. Rowan was glad to pass the baton, but holding the little guy hadn't been so bad. Not really.

"Come on, buddy. It's chow time." He carried Noah into the dining room, where Louanne had their dinner waiting.

She lifted the tray on the high chair, then, after Rowan put Noah on the torn vinyl seat, she secured the baby and replaced the chrome tray.

After putting a ladle of beans and a chunk of ham into a small plastic bowl, she took a fork and made mush out of the contents. "Let Mama mash the air out of these beans for you."

Rowan laughed. "You've got to be kidding. You think smashing beans to a paste will get rid of whatever causes gas?"

Louanne cast him a bright-eyed smile that surpassed any he'd seen her sister flash on magazine covers. "No, of course not. But my mom used to say that when we were kids. And I'm finding myself doing and saying a lot of the same things."

"Like what?" he asked.

"Like 'skin-a-rabbit' when I lift his shirt over his head." She shrugged. "Just silly little things like that."

Rowan didn't remember his mother. *Only that*

she'd had dark hair, like his. He paused, his fork in midair.

"What's the matter?" Louanne asked.

He wasn't sure. But an uneasy feeling settled around him. His mother had been young and pretty. But she hadn't been a part of his life. He looked at Louanne, saw the concern on her face. "I lost my mom. I don't know how. But she wasn't there for me when I was a kid."

Her lips parted, and compassion flared in her eyes. "I'm sorry."

"Yeah. Me, too. I guess." Remorse settled in his gut. Was this what he could expect as his memory came back—bits and pieces of stuff he'd rather forget?

Not ready to dig up more about his mother or her loss, Rowan turned the conversation back on something safe. "Where's Noah's dad?"

All signs of the happy face he'd seen earlier vanished, and Louanne sat up straight in her chair like a well-versed princess. "He's dead."

Rowan didn't know what he'd expected her to say. That the guy ran off, but sent a child support check on a monthly basis. That Noah had the benefit of a father, even if the man didn't live in the same house. Kids needed a dad who took part in their lives, who loved them.

Still, even though children might need a father, not all of them were fortunate enough to have one. Rowan knew that for a fact. And not just because his sister had mentioned it to Louanne, who had, in turn, passed that tidbit of information along to him.

His dad hadn't ever been there for him, either.

The realization gripped his heart, squeezing out a surge of resentment. Had his father ever loved him? Appreciated him? Been proud of him? It didn't seem like it.

He had an overwhelming suspicion that his father never had cared about him.

But not all men were like that, were they? Didn't some guys love their kids? Look forward to being with them and asking about their day?

He glanced at the baby who'd smeared beans all over his face. In spite of the mess, Rowan found himself smiling at the little guy. "Did Noah's dad get a chance to see his son?"

"No." She glanced down at her bowl, stirred the beans rather than scoop them up with her spoon.

Louanne didn't know how the conversation had switched so quickly to *her* memories. And she wasn't sure how to change the subject back to one that was easier to talk about—safer.

Lying didn't come easy to her. Of course, that hadn't stopped her from fabricating an exciting past, like she'd done when she first stepped foot on the small but prestigious campus of Cedar Glen.

At the time, she'd been determined to shed her backwoods image. And Louanne Brown had seemed like such a plain, going-nowhere name. So, following her sister's lead, she legally changed her name. Lanay Landers was far more fitting and held the promise of an exciting, new life.

It hadn't seemed like that big of a deal, but her father had been hurt. She'd promised to change it back, but hadn't gotten around to it before she received news of the plane crash.

"How did he die?"

Her dad? Rowan's question caught her off guard, and it took a moment to realize he was talking about Noah's father.

Why wouldn't he let this subject die? She hated to perpetuate the tales she'd told. And she hadn't had to lie very often, since she avoided going into Austin, where Richard would probably focus his search for her.

She'd been ashamed of the small, hick town in which she'd grown up. So she'd told everyone at Cedar Glen that she was from Austin and implied that she was a sophisticated city girl.

"I'd rather not talk about it," she told Rowan, fighting the urge to concoct yet another lie she would then have to remember.

He nodded, then dug into his bowl. Moments later, he looked up. "Did your parents get a chance to see the baby?"

"No. They died before he was born." She wasn't sure how honest she wanted to be, since she'd kept things so close to the vest for so long. Not even Aggie and Pete knew everything. And bless them, they'd been kind enough not to pry, especially since she'd let them think she was embarrassed to be an unwed mother.

"It must be lonely out here for you."

She nodded. It was. And not a day went by that she didn't wish her parents were still here, that they could enjoy their grandson and watch him grow. That she could apologize for hurting them, even though that had never been her intent. Regret and remorse muscled to the forefront, stealing her appetite.

Memories of her parents, of her boring childhood lingered in this house, which in some ways had been good. She'd come to grips with her past, with her roots.

But she still felt guilty for not being happy with whom she'd been, for being ashamed of her humble childhood. For not being more appreciative. And especially for not being a better daughter.

Guilt, she supposed, was a penance she'd pay for the rest of her life.

It was too late to apologize to her parents, now that they were gone. Too late to admit how badly she felt about not appreciating their dream, even though it was so different from her own that, once upon a time, she'd thought her parents didn't dream at all.

She'd been wrong, though. Wrong about so many things.

But maybe by encouraging Rowan to return home and make peace with his dad—something she would never have the chance to do—she could find vindication.

Of course, Rowan would have to remember who he was and where he came from first.

For a moment, she didn't like the idea of him leaving, of her having to face her own sorry life alone. But it was for the best. At least, it would be better for him.

She looked at Rowan and tried to conjure sincerity to mask her lie. "Am I lonely? Not really. I like the tranquility and simplicity that the Lazy B provides. And I can't think of living anywhere else." In a way, she supposed it was true.

But the reality of her desolate future seemed to suck the breath right out of her.

Louanne kissed Noah, then placed him into his crib. "Good night, sweet baby."

He fussed momentarily, not ready to end his day, but within moments, he'd popped his thumb in his mouth and laid his head upon the mattress.

As she made her way back to the living room, where Rowan waited, she looked forward to having company. There wasn't much to do in the evenings, especially since Louanne had given up reading. Watching television, of course, had become a comfortable routine, but at this time of the year, there were mainly reruns airing. So, in a way, playing cards with Pete and Aggie was actually something to look forward to, particularly since her days were long, the work endless.

For a woman who'd been geared for a life of academia until her novel scored big, running a cattle ranch had been a daunting task. Thank goodness she had Pete and Aggie to help. She didn't know how she would have made it without the aging ranch foreman and his wife.

"Is Noah asleep?" Rowan asked, from his seat on the edge of the beige vinyl recliner.

"Not yet. But he will be in a minute or two. He's had a big day today. Those afternoon walks always wear him down."

"I can understand why. He got pretty wound up, just pointing at things." Rowan chuckled. "He would lurch and move in my arms, kind of like a kid in a swing set pumping for momentum, to show me where he wanted to go."

Louanne smiled. "He's trying so hard to communicate."

"I noticed." The man who'd once been uneasy with babies grinned like an old hand. "He'll probably be talking up a storm in no time at all."

She placed her hands on her hips and arched, trying to stretch out the ache in her back that never seemed to go away. Her body had gone through a lot of changes in the past year or so, first with pregnancy and childbirth, then with the physical demands of life on a working cattle ranch.

They didn't have as many cattle as before, which was just as well. They couldn't afford another hired hand, other than Pete. The ranch was dying; they both knew it. And she suspected the only reason Pete hadn't retired was out of concern and loyalty to her.

"Is there something I can do to help?" Rowan stood, letting her know he was willing to set up or whatever.

Louanne smiled. "Knowing Aggie, she'll bring everything we need, other than a pot of coffee."

"You mean the goodies she talked about?"

"Let me put it this way. Pete's the one who will need some help lugging things over here."

Just then a light rap sounded at the screen door, and they both turned to see Pete carrying a card table and a platter of cookies. "Is the baby asleep?"

"If not, he's close to it." Louanne swung open the door and took the plate from his steady but craggy hands. "Where's Aggie?"

"She's packing Noah's wagon with the rest of the stuff and should be here shortly."

Thirty minutes later, the four of them sat around the card table, as Rowan learned the intricacies and strategies of *Schazam,* a game played with kitchen spoons, three dice and matchsticks.

When the older woman had mentioned playing cards, Rowan's first thought was poker. But when she'd arrived pulling a child's red wagon packed full of home-baked sweets, he'd been surprised to see her whip out three decks of cards, dice and a box of matches.

"Schazam!" Pete shouted, as he threw down four tens and snatched a teaspoon from the middle of the table.

Aggie clapped her hands, then gave her husband a high five. Rowan couldn't help but laugh. Playing cards with Pete and Aggie wasn't at all what he'd expected.

Rowan's idea of cards was a group of guys, the curl of cigar smoke and a warm swig of bourbon as it slid down the throat. Coarse language that always seemed to hit the heart of a matter. Big belly laughs. Friendly bickering and banter. And not to mention, the wealth of knowledge a young man learned from men nearly twice his age.

Rowan played cards with older men.

And he'd always looked forward to it. Looked forward to the priceless words of wisdom people didn't find in books.

A man don't need friends when he's got the world by the balls and his pockets full of cash. He needs 'em when he's down and out. That's when you find out who your real friends are, son.

Son.

Grief surged in his chest, although he wasn't exactly sure why.

"Son, it's your deal." Pete passed the triple-deck of cards to Rowan.

Upon the transfer of the stack, Rowan felt the warmth of Pete's touch. Felt the years of wear on the cards. Sensed the camaraderie between the others at the table.

It seemed obvious that the older couple and the mother and child had become a family of sorts. And it was touching. Is that what Rowan grieved? Not having a closeness like that? Or was it just the blasted amnesia that made him feel as though no one gave a damn about him?

He hated not knowing. Not understanding.

"You sure you'll be okay while we're gone?" Aggie asked Louanne. "We can cancel our plans."

"I wouldn't hear of it." The young woman reached across the table with work-roughened hands. Gentle hands that deserved the luxury of a weekly manicure.

"Where are you going?" Rowan asked the older couple.

"We're gonna take a trip to Amarillo to see Aggie's sister. Then on up to Colorado." Pete leaned back in his chair and looked at Rowan. "You ever see that part of the country?"

"No." The answer just seemed to pop out, so Rowan assumed it was true. But hell, he really didn't know for sure where he'd traveled.

"I haven't been to visit my sister in close to ten years," Aggie said. "We do a lot of writing and talking on the telephone. But it's not the same."

Pete took a swig from a chipped, blue coffee mug. "We bought us a used RV from a widow woman east of Austin. But I sure wish we had a fancy Winnebago like Doc Haines just bought."

"The one we have is just fine. We don't need anything fancy." Aggie patted the top of Louanne's hand. "You'll have to come see what I've done to that ol' motor home. I've got it all cleaned up. And I made new curtains and a couple of throw pillows for the sofa."

"Did you get a chance to see Doc's Winnebago?" Pete asked Louanne. "Before he took off, he gave me a tour."

"No, I didn't look inside."

"It's a nice one. And it's got all the modern conveniences." Pete glanced at Aggie and slid her a smile. "But you're right, Sugar. The one we've got will work just fine."

Aggie reached for one of the peanut butter squares Rowan favored, a rich chewy cookie bar that melted in the mouth. "I'm really looking forward to getting away, but I'm sure going to miss Noah. I don't suppose you'd let us take him with us? We'll just be gone a week."

The attractive young mother smiled, "He's a handful, and if I wouldn't miss him something fierce, I'd let him go. I know he'd be in good hands with you."

"The only thing holding us back is you," Pete told Louanne. "We hate leaving you out here to fend for yourself."

"I'll be all right. Besides, you two need a vacation."

"Don't worry," Rowan said, as he handed Pete the

stack of cards to cut. "I'll stick around and help out until you get back—if Louanne will tell me what to do."

"That does make us feel a lot better." The older man separated the cards in three groups, making the cut. "You sure you don't mind?"

"No, not at all." In fact, Rowan would look forward to feeling useful, to feeling as though he had some kind of purpose. Especially since he had no place to go.

Each time he tried to access his memory, he found himself fumbling in the dark. Except for the bits that flashed like lightning here and there.

Thirty minutes and three bellows of "Schazam!" later, Pete and Aggie took the empty wagon back home. They'd left behind nearly a dozen chocolate chip cookies, a quarter of an apple pie and several peanut butter squares, much to Rowan's delight.

He popped another one into his mouth, then picked up the empty mugs and carried them into the kitchen.

Louanne followed behind with the plates of left-over sweets. "I can get the dishes, Rowan. You don't need to help."

"It's time I started pulling my own weight." He plugged the sink and turned on the hot water.

Louanne reached for a plastic bottle of dish soap. "If I had to face the remains of Thanksgiving dinner, I could understand. But it's only four mugs, a coffeepot and a few pieces of flatware."

"Maybe I like being with you," he said, watching her eyes light up and a little color warm her cheeks.

She turned away, quickly washing the few dishes, rinsing them and placing them on the rack.

Rowan used a clean but frayed dishtowel to dry them, yet all the while, he couldn't keep his eyes off her, couldn't keep from studying her classic profile, her turned-up nose. The dark spikes of her lashes.

Was it her down-home, earthy beauty that drew him to her? Or was it merely the fact that she lit up one dark corner in his world?

"That's it." She turned off the water and dried her hands, then walked toward the kitchen door.

He merely stood there, watching her.

This woman didn't belong on a run-down cattle ranch. Didn't belong in worn jeans and faded cowboy shirts. She belonged in linen and pearls. And he longed to see her in classy clothes, in a different setting.

"What's the matter?" she asked, eyes still bright, cheeks still flushed.

"Nothing." He approached her.

A whiff of her wildflower scent triggered a hunger. A need. And his longing took on a different slant. He wanted to touch her again, to pull her into his arms. To feel her flush against him.

He brushed a loose strand of hair from her cheek, and her lips parted.

To stop him? To reprimand him for wanting to kiss her again? Or had it been a natural response to what she surely knew he intended to do?

He placed a finger on her chin, tilting her face to

his. When she didn't step back, didn't pull away, he kissed her—slow and easy at first, brushing his lips against hers.

As her mouth opened, he deepened the kiss until their tongues mated, until he knew every nook and cranny of her warm, silky mouth and suspected she knew his as well.

Had he ever enjoyed a kiss so much? He doubted it, cursing the darkness that wouldn't allow his memories to surface.

As his hands roamed her back and slipped to the soft contour of her hips, she pulled away. "That wasn't a very good idea."

It had seemed like an awfully good idea to him. It still did. And he suspected she liked it every bit as much as he did. "What's so bad about kissing?"

She seemed to struggle with the answer. Or maybe with the reason. "Kissing leads to other things. And I'm not ready for that."

"Are you missing Noah's father?" he asked, assuming she still grieved for the man who'd last made love to her.

"No. Believe it or not, I'm not missing him at all."

Was that bad? Is that what bothered her? That she no longer grieved for the loss of her son's father?

Then she flipped off the light switch, leaving Rowan in the dark.

Chapter Six

The next morning, Rowan and Louanne sat at the kitchen table, eating scrambled eggs and ham.

From the time they'd awakened and ran into each other in the hall, their conversation had been bland and generic, like "Did you sleep well?" and "Yes, thank you."

On the outside, everything appeared friendly and normal. But inside, Rowan felt as awkward as a 49er linebacker in a tutu. And he suspected Louanne wasn't any more comfortable than that.

Several times, he'd thought about mentioning the kiss they'd shared last night. But he hadn't.

For some reason, Louanne hadn't wanted to go into detail about her reservations. Or about her past.

And he needed to respect that. After all, who better than Rowan understood a person's right to privacy?

His memory sputtered again, releasing another revelation that didn't open any big doors in his mind.

Rowan kept his feelings to himself.

He jabbed his fork at a chunk of ham, wishing he could do something to still the clumsy silence. But as long as he and Louanne were the only two sitting here, the kiss would linger between them.

"When do you expect Noah to wake up?" he asked.

"He's sleeping later than usual because he was so fretful last night."

The poor kid had been fussy? Rowan must have slept through it all, and for some reason, it made him feel like a jerk for not being aware of the child's discomfort or the nocturnal activity. But hell, what kind of help would he have been able to offer? He didn't know jack squat about babies.

"I didn't hear anything," Rowan said.

"Good. I tried to get to him before he woke you. His twelve-month molars have been bothering him, especially at night, so I took him outside on the porch. That seemed to help, especially since the rocking chair is on the blink."

Before Rowan could respond, Noah cried out. "Ma! Ma! Me!"

Louanne smiled, probably as eager as Rowan was to have a diversion, stood and carried her plate to the sink.

"Sounds like he's awake and raring to go."

"You've got that right," she said. "I'd better get him. Will you excuse me?"

"Sure." Rowan was glad Noah would be joining them, since their conversation wouldn't be as stilted.

They both continued to tap dance around the blood-stirring kisses they'd shared, as well as their secrets—the memories amnesia had locked away from him and the thoughts Louanne kept under wraps.

He didn't know whether his poker playing skills had made him good at reading people or not, but there was far more to Louanne Brown than met the eye. And he'd bet the farm on that.

A few moments later, Louanne returned with the pudgy, pajama-clad baby boy. Noah brightened at the sight of Rowan and squealed in delight.

Imagine that. The kid actually liked him. Had anyone ever seemed that happy to see him before? He doubted it.

A gush of warmth swelled in Rowan's chest, and he shot the kid a sappy smile. "Hey, pal. Did those nasty chompers give you fits last night?"

Noah grinned in response, then lurched toward the high chair and grunted.

Without needing to be asked, Rowan lifted the chrome tray and waited for Louanne to secure the child in his seat before locking the tray back into place.

"How about some milk?" Louanne asked her son.

Noah smiled, revealing four little teeth, and

plopped his pudgy hands on his reflection in the chrome. "Muh."

Rowan took another sip of coffee and watched Louanne pour milk into a yellow plastic cup with two handles on the side.

A sharp rap sounded at the back door, then Pete entered the house through the service porch. "I could smell that coffee brewing clear out in the south pasture, so I decided to take a little break."

"Good morning," Louanne told the aging foreman. "Come on in and help yourself."

"Thanks." Pete took an olive-green mug from the cupboard and filled it with the rich brew. Then he turned and leaned against the pink tile countertop. "Aggie and I had a good time last night."

"So did we." Louanne glanced at Rowan, as if looking for confirmation.

He nodded, since he'd enjoyed himself, too. And not just because of the camaraderie. He found Pete and Aggie entertaining—in a television sitcom sort of way. He'd been reminded of an affectionate Fred and Ethel Mertz. And more than once, he had to bite his tongue to keep from laughing at their antics.

Yet at the same time, there was something special about the couple. Something down-to-earth and real. And Rowan suspected Pete and Aggie were the kind of people a man could count on in a pinch.

Of course, he'd never been one to share sentiments like that. Doing so left him too vulnerable.

Another little tidbit of his past busted free. Why did he want to protect himself and his feelings? Was that a result of the amnesia that plagued him? Or of something in his past?

"Schazam is a great game," Pete said. "But I'm partial to poker."

"Do you play very often?" Rowan wondered whether he'd be invited to join in and hoped he would.

"Nope. I'm afraid not." Pete took another sip of coffee. "It's not easy rustling up enough guys around here to make the stakes interesting."

Again, Rowan tried to conjure a memory of his poker-playing past, but didn't have much luck. He did suspect that Pete would fit right in with his old buddies—especially if he liked interesting stakes.

Pete would fit right in with his old poker cronies— men with more common sense than wealth, class or education.

Great. If that were the case, why couldn't Rowan remember who those old cronies were? Not even one name or face came to mind.

Pete furrowed his bushy, gray brow and stepped closer to Rowan. "That wound seems to be mending pretty good. When is Doc going to take the stitches out?"

Louanne wiped a dribble of milk from Noah's chin. "Doc said he'd stop by on his way home this weekend."

The discussion of Rowan's wound reminded him of the accident and the motorcycle that had landed in a ditch. And since his family had already been no-tified, he suspected it was probably locked up in some impound yard by now.

"By the way, Pete. I need to get my bike and bring it back to the ranch. I'm sure you're pretty busy, but I could use some help, if you can spare some time."

"I'll be glad to go with you." The craggy-faced cowboy took a last swig of coffee, then set the mug on the countertop. "Maybe together we can get it into the back of the truck and bring it here."

"How bad did it look?" Rowan asked.

"It shouldn't be too hard to get her running, but it'll probably cost a bundle to get her looking good as new. From what I've heard, those Harleys are ex-pensive to buy and to fix."

Awareness nudged Rowan. He hadn't given the motorcycle much thought before, and he wasn't en-tirely sure why he hadn't. But the bike *was* a Harley. And it had cost him a near fortune to buy before he added all the extras.

He sure hoped the accident hadn't caused too much damage, because the Harley Fat Boy had be-come a part of him. Almost like a friend.

His only friend?

A fresh surge of grief settled around him, and a vision fluttered in his mind. A grave on the hillside of a cemetery. A twenty-one gun salute. A flag being folded and handed to him. A lump in his throat the size of Mt. Whitney.

But the image vanished as quickly as it had formed.

"Your sister said someone notified them that the bike had been found," Louanne said. "So it may not be lying in that ditch any longer."

"Well, let's go take a look-see," Pete suggested. "And if it's gone, we can talk to Sheriff McDonald. I'll take time to help you out this morning."

"I appreciate it." Rowan watched as Louanne stood from her seat at the table, walked to the sink and poured out the rest of her coffee. He studied the way the worn denim stretched across her rounded hips and wondered why she didn't wear something more feminine. Something more likely to show off the womanly curves she hid.

"Do you and Noah want to ride with us?" Rowan figured the baby would probably enjoy getting out and seeing some scenery.

"We'll pass. Aggie and I are going to can string beans today." She placed her mug on the countertop, then used a spatula to remove a small scoop of scrambled eggs from the cast iron skillet on the stove and place it in Noah's plastic bowl. "But thanks for thinking of us."

Moments later, as the men made their way to the dirty, white Ford pickup, Pete opened the driver's door, but didn't climb inside. Instead, he peered across the seat at Rowan. "Louanne doesn't like leaving the ranch. Aggie and I have tried to get her to go into town with us, but she won't."

That didn't seem natural. The women Rowan knew loved to go places, to shop. To get dressed up and go to parties. Not waste away on a ranch in the middle of nowhere.

Of course, Louanne wasn't like any of the women he knew. He wasn't sure how he'd come to that conclusion, but for some reason, it just *seemed* to be true.

"Aggie thinks Louanne has that fear of leaving the house," Pete added. "You ever hear about folks who suffer from that?"

Rowan nodded. He'd heard about that kind of anxiety. But he wasn't so sure that was Louanne's problem, although he didn't know why he felt that way. Maybe because she seemed to be such a complex woman—a woman who held back what she was really thinking and feeling.

They drove to the place where Pete had spotted Rowan's motorcycle. But the bike was no longer in the ditch that separated the long stretch of county road from the barbwire boundary of the Lazy B.

"Louanne was right," Pete said. "Someone hauled it off. Let's head into town. We can talk to the sheriff and ask where it is."

"Are you sure that you have the time? I don't want to keep you from your work."

"Hell, I'll make time." Pete chuckled to himself. "Then I'll put you to work so you can help me catch up."

"That sounds like a great deal to me." Rowan actually relished the idea of physical labor, of a good, hard workout—but for more reasons than the exercise. Helping out on the ranch would make him feel like a contributor, rather than a taker. "I'll be happy to work for my room and board."

For some reason, Rowan liked the idea of settling in Pebble Creek. And even though he wanted to get his memory back, he had no intention of returning to California.

But he'd be damned if he knew why.

In the kitchen, Aggie and Louanne sat across the antique oak table from each other, snapping green beans and preparing them for canning.

Noah entertained himself in the secondhand play-pen that Aggie had found at a garage sale. He gummed a pacifier like it was an old stogie and grunted or squealed periodically, entertaining the two women with his baby-sweet antics.

"Sharing the workload makes canning a whole lot easier," Aggie said.

"It sure does." Louanne cast a smile at the older woman. In the last eighteen months, Aggie had become a dear friend. And having her around made a tough, lonely life bearable.

Aggie grabbed another handful of beans from the strainer and began to snap them. "When is Doc coming back from his vacation?"

"He hoped to come back on Saturday afternoon and mentioned coming by here to check on Rowan."

"Good." Aggie tossed a handful of snapped beans into the bowl. "I hope you plan to talk to Doc about your feelings."

Her feelings? For Rowan? Was her attraction to the man that obvious?

Aggie added, "I was hoping Doc would give you a prescription that will make you feel better about leaving the house."

Louanne was at a crossroads. She had to either perpetuate the false assumption or confess.

Did she dare tell Aggie the truth? Admit that her fear and anxiety couldn't be helped by medication?

Louanne believed the fewer people who knew she'd come home to the Lazy B, the better. But the reason for her return had been a heavy burden to carry alone.

"Pete and I kept your secret," Aggie said. "No one in Pebble Creek knows you've come home with a baby. But I think you're afraid of more than gossip."

Louanne stared at the green beans in her hand.

Undaunted by the silence, Aggie continued to drive home her point. "It's not healthy for a pretty, young woman like you to hole up here at the ranch."

Maybe not, but Louanne felt safer here than anywhere. "I appreciate your concern, Aggie, but I'm getting some much-needed rest. College life became very stressful for me, and I like the slower pace."

"College was too stressful?" Aggie lifted a silver-gray brow. "For a smart bookworm like you?"

Okay, so Louanne would have to come up with another, more plausible excuse. But since Louanne wasn't particularly keen on feigning an anxiety she didn't have, maybe she ought to level with her friend.

After all, Aggie had proved to be trustworthy on more than one occasion. And after nearly a year and a half, Richard hadn't found her yet. If she were lucky, another graduate student might have caught his eye—although that was a disturbing thought. She wouldn't wish Richard Keith on her worst enemy.

"I haven't been truthful with you," Louanne confessed. "There's a whole lot more to the story."

"You don't feel as though you can confide in me?" Both the tone of Aggie's voice and her cocker spaniel eyes revealed the depth of her disappointment.

"When I explain, maybe you'll understand why I kept things a secret. But you'll need to promise not to tell anyone. Not even Pete."

Aggie paused momentarily, as though weighing what the agreement might cost her. The older couple loved each other, and Louanne doubted there was much they didn't share.

"All right." Aggie placed her elbows on the table and leaned forward. "I'll keep your secret, even from Pete."

Now what? Louanne had opened the door to the basement of her fears. Did she have the courage to step into the dark? To confront what frightened her the most?

She took a deep breath, then started at the beginning. Or pretty close to the beginning. "Two years ago, I began dating one of my professors at college. He was an older man and the epitome of class and charm. I found myself falling for him, and when he asked me out, I agreed."

"Is that ethical?" Aggie reached for a handful of green beans. "You know, a teacher dating a student?"

"No. I suppose it isn't. But I was very close to finishing my doctorate coursework and ready to start my dissertation in English. We were both adults. And we were very discreet."

"I assume that man was Noah's father."

Louanne nodded, finding it hard to voice the truth out loud.

"How did he die? I've been curious, but you always changed the subject whenever I brought it up."

"He didn't die. Unfortunately, the man is very much alive."

Aggie's hands froze, and she dropped the green beans she'd been holding. "What do you mean, *'unfortunately'?*"

"Over time, Richard became increasingly possessive. He began to follow me. And whenever I wasn't someplace he thought I should be, he would accuse me of seeing someone else. Someone younger."

"I assume you weren't," Aggie said.

"Of course not. But he'd been masking a serious drinking problem, and as it became more and more apparent, I realized my mistake and naïveté in getting involved with him. But I knew I had to be careful how I ended things." Louanne took a deep breath, then blew it out slowly. "One day, he broke into my apartment while I was at the library doing research. When I returned home, he accused me of cheating on him. I tried to deny it, but he threw me against the wall. Then he struck me."

"Did you call the police?"

"I probably should have, but he began to cry. And he told me he was sorry. That he loved me so much, it made him crazy."

"All those wife beaters say they're sorry," Aggie said. "But the abuse just gets worse."

"I'm aware of that. But I was just months away from completing work on my doctorate, and I planned to stick it out."

"Things got worse, didn't they?"

Louanne blew out a ragged sigh. "Richard was twenty years older than me and had never had a child. I'm not sure he'd ever wanted one, but he got this weird idea about a baby of ours having a genetic predisposition to intelligence and perfection. A wonder kid."

"That's almost scary," Aggie said. "Planning like that takes the miracle out of birth."

"I agree. But having a child with me became an

obsession. He began checking into private nursery schools for gifted children. And the more he pushed for a child, the more I insisted he use condoms." Louanne glanced at her friend, hoping she understood the dilemma she faced.

"I guess God had other ideas." Aggie glanced at Noah, her eyes beaming with love and admiration. "Look at what a precious little boy you have."

"You're right." Noah was precious. And he was a blessing Louanne had never anticipated in those early months while Richard haunted her waking hours, and not just her sleep.

For the hundredth time, Louanne whispered a prayer, asking God to forgive her for not wanting the baby and wishing she'd miscarry. She'd actually contemplated an abortion, although just for a moment. But she couldn't go through with it.

Still, the fact she'd never wanted Noah tormented her each time she looked into her son's sweet little face.

Louanne took a deep breath, then slowly let it out. "One night, after Richard had been drinking more than usual, he confessed to having poked holes in the condoms we'd been using. To make matters worse, I then found out I was pregnant. And that's when I began to plot a careful escape that couldn't wait until I finished school."

"How did you do that?"

"I covered my tracks, or at least I hope I did. Several weeks before running away, I changed my address so that the entire college computer system reflected a bogus home residence in Austin, which is where I'd told everyone I was from." Louanne stood and moved aimlessly about the kitchen, restless. Uneasy. "I also took the paper files from the English department, just in case Richard thought to look there. And I destroyed them."

"Then you ran away?"

"That was the plan. Richard had a night class, but for some reason, he canceled it and came to my place unexpectedly. He found a suitcase on the bed." Louanne closed her eyes, remembering that night. "His eyes grew wild, and I thought he was going to go into another rage. I told him that I had to go home, that my grandmother was seriously ill. I must have been convincing, because he let me go."

"Does the man know he has a son?"

"No." Louanne swallowed hard, remembering Richard's threat, as he watched her go.

I'll see you back in my bed, willing to have my baby, or in a casket, six feet under.

"And so you came home in secret," Aggie said. "That's why you won't go into town."

Louanne nodded. She'd done everything she could think of to protect herself and Noah from the professor. She told Doc Haines that she wanted to have her baby at home, just like her mother had done. She'd also made Doc promise not to tell anyone in town that she'd come back or had a baby. And she'd refused to put the father's name on Noah's birth certificate.

Richard had said he'd follow her to the ends of the earth, which is exactly where she always believed the Lazy B had been located. And so she'd come home with her tail between her legs, pregnant and licking her wounds.

Aggie stood, and when she reached out her arms, Louanne eased into her embrace and absorbed every ounce of comfort her friend offered.

"I'll keep your secret," Aggie said. "And Pete and I won't let anything happen to you or to Noah. You'll be safe here."

Louanne certainly hoped so. But she could never be sure. The more people who knew her secret made the risk of Richard finding her all that more real.

And even though she told herself that she'd given Richard the slip, she walked on eggshells every day of her life, fearing that someday he would find her.

And, even worse, find his son.

There wasn't much in the small town of Pebble Creek, just a couple of shops on the main drag. Mabel's Diner. Farley's Fine Clothing. The Creekside General Store.

Rowan didn't suppose the community had much to offer, so maybe that's why Louanne didn't venture off the ranch. But for some reason, he didn't believe that was the case.

Pete parked the truck in front of the sheriff's office, and they both went inside. It didn't take long to find out the bike had, indeed, been hauled away.

After Sheriff McDonald explained the impound fees, which needed to be paid in cash or with a cashier's check, he gave them directions to the lot where they could find the Harley.

The men headed for the pickup. As Rowan reached the passenger door, something caught his eye. "Just a minute, Pete."

He bypassed the pickup, crossed the street and headed toward Farley's Fine Clothing.

"What you got in mind to do?" Pete asked, tagging along behind him.

"I want to get something for Louanne. Something to show my appreciation for her taking me in and tending my wounds."

"That'd be nice. My woman loves surprises." Pete lifted his worn, black cowboy hat and adjusted it on his head. "It might be hard for you to believe, seeing as how Louanne doesn't do much primping anymore, but she and her sister used to get all gussied up when they were young girls."

Apparently, Tallulah still liked to wear stylish clothes. But he wondered what had triggered the change in Louanne's wardrobe. Lack of money? The death of her parents? Childbirth?

The death of her old lover?

She'd told Rowan she didn't miss the man at all.

Had that been a lie? Or had she never loved the man who'd fathered her baby?

It was hard to say. But Rowan was determined to see the tall, attractive brunette "all gussied up" again.

He went straight for a rack of dresses and began to sort through the various colors and styles. When he pulled out a lime-green sundress in a slinky fabric, he whipped it around for Pete to see. "What do you think about this?"

Pete let out a slow whistle. "It's pretty. And it ought to look real nice on Louanne. 'Course, she doesn't go anywhere and probably won't wear it."

"She can wear it around the house." A smile crept onto Rowan's face. *She could wear it for him.*

And he would make her feel good about herself. Good enough to go out in public again. Then he would take her into town for a night of dinner and dancing.

It would be a piece of cake, a walk in the park. A slam dunk.

Rowan was a charmer. And he'd never had a lady he was interested in turn down one of his offers. No matter what it happened to be.

Now that was a revelation that would prove to be useful.

His smile deepened. He would charm Louanne Brown into another blood-pumping, mind-spinning kiss.

And this time, instead of regret, he would see those golden-brown eyes light up with a smile.

Chapter Seven

Louanne stood before the white, sturdy, hulk of a stove and carefully removed mason jars filled with green beans from a pot of boiling water.

At the sound of the pickup returning home, Aggie peered out the kitchen window. "It's Pete and Rowan. And they must have found the motorcycle. I see something black in the back of the truck."

Louanne stepped away from the heat and joined Aggie at the window. A smile tugged at her lips, as she watched the men scratch their heads, then try to maneuver the bike out of the truck and into the barn.

"Pete's always loved tinkering with engines and

things. So I have a feeling, he'll want to help get that motorcycle running again. I sure hope that contraption doesn't give my fool husband any wild ideas. Years ago, he wanted to buy a big old Yamaha and put me on the back." Aggie chuckled. "Now, do I look like one of those biker chicks?"

Louanne smiled at the thought of lanky Pete and his heavyset wife riding down the road, the wind whipping their gray hair. Letting themselves go, feeling free and young again.

It sounded like great fun to Louanne. And she could certainly see herself perched on the Harley behind Rowan, her arms wrapped around his waist, her breasts pressed against his broad back, her legs straddling a powerful motorcycle. Just the thought was exhilarating, liberating.

But daydreaming like that was a complete waste of time. Especially with her experience.

Her one and only relationship had been with a man she hadn't really known. A man with secrets he didn't initially reveal—like his excessive drinking, his need for domination and control. His penchant for violence and threats.

Louanne certainly didn't need to repeat that foolish mistake. Especially since Rowan was as much a stranger to himself as he was to her.

She just wished she didn't find him so darn handsome, his eyes so mesmerizing. His kiss so stimulating.

But no matter how attractive the man was, no matter how much she enjoyed his kiss, she couldn't let herself go.

She *wouldn't*.

Ten minutes later, the men entered the house through the service porch, chuckling about something, and joined Aggie and Luanne in the kitchen.

Pete scanned the room. "Where's Noah? Taking a nap?"

Aggie shushed her husband. "Keep your voice down. We don't want him waking up yet."

That was true. As precious and entertaining as Noah could be under normal situations, he woke up like a little grizzly bear if he didn't get enough sleep.

But it wasn't Pete who caught Louanne's eye, who drew her attention. Who caused her blood to warm.

Louanne's gaze settled on Rowan, on his vibrant eyes, on the boyish smile that lit the room. On the way he filled out her father's shirt and jeans. He balanced a grocery bag in one arm and a smaller one in his free hand.

"What's that?" she asked, her eyes focusing on the cream-colored bag with a red Farley's logo in his hands. Apparently, he'd gone shopping, which shouldn't surprise her. He'd probably gotten tired of wearing her father's hand-me-downs.

Rowan smiled a bit sheepishly, while Pete grinned from ear to ear.

"What's so funny?" Louanne asked.

"Nothing." Pete looked at Rowan and nodded toward the smaller bag. "You gonna give it to her?"

"In front of a crowd? I was going to wait until we were alone, but I guess it won't hurt to let her have it now." Rowan set the grocery bag on the counter, then handed the beige bag to Louanne.

She furrowed her brow, then looked at Rowan for an explanation. When he didn't give her one, she asked, "What's this?"

"It's a gift." He tossed her a crooked grin. "For you."

Aggie edged closer, her curiosity apparent. "What's in it?"

There was only one way to find out. The crisp paper crinkled as Louanne opened the bag and peeked inside. A pretty lime-green fabric caught her eye. Curiosity mounting, she withdrew a slinky sundress.

It was the kind of garment she might have worn years ago—back when she'd actually hoped to make her mark on the world, when she'd wanted to turn a man's head. When she'd wanted to be noticed and appreciated.

"I don't understand." She looked at the gorgeous man who was proving to be unpredictable. Would he explain?

He merely stood there, watching her every move. "What's this for?" she asked.

"I wanted to thank you for taking me in." Rowan slipped his thumbs into the front pockets of his worn jeans, looking as gorgeous and devilish as ever. "Do you like it?"

Like it? Of course, she did. It was lovely. But what in the world was she going to do with a fancy garment like that on a cattle ranch? Her days of dressing up were over.

Apparently, her silence implied she hadn't appreciated his thoughtfulness or the gift, because he sobered and took the bag from her hands, leaving her to hold the dress. Then he reached into his pocket and withdrew a slip of paper. "I kept the receipt. So you can exchange it for something else, if you want to."

"No. I mean yes." Louanne fingered the cloth, the chafed skin of her hands snagging on the silky material. Then she looked at Rowan. "It's pretty. Thank you for thinking of me."

"But?" he asked, picking up on her reservations.

"I'm not sure where I'd wear it."

"Why don't you wear it while you hang out the wash? Or—" he nodded at the countertop where a dozen jars cooled "—or while you can green beans?"

"That seems frivolous. Don't you think?"

"Not at all." Their gazes locked, and for a moment, the walls of the room closed in, leaving only the two of them to deal with a blood-rushing attraction.

As crazy as the idea seemed, Louanne was sorely tempted to slip into the stylish dress. To do her hair and apply some lipstick and a bit of mascara. Maybe even give herself a manicure and a pedicure. And even more tempting was the thought of Rowan's re-action if she put some effort into it.

Because truthfully speaking and humility aside, Louanne could look every bit as glamorous as her sister, Tallulah, when she wanted to.

Lanay Landers, the stylish, sophisticated identity she'd banished to the far corner of her memory, reared her head, daring her to dress up for Rowan. To feel like a sexually attractive lady one more time.

But she brushed aside the irrational suggestion. "It seems silly to keep a dress I'll only wear to can beans and hang out the wash."

Rowan's smile returned, and his gaze pierced hers. "How about wearing it tonight? For dinner? We can feed Noah, then dine on the front porch."

Dine? He made it sound fancy, special. Appealing. And the idea held more merit than Louanne cared to admit.

Especially since she wondered what Rowan would think of the woman she no longer was.

That evening, Louanne wiped the colorful remnants of Noah's chicken-and-rice dinner from his little face and hands, then removed him from his high chair.

She wasn't sure how Rowan had managed to talk her into eating with him on the front porch. But he had. And she'd agreed to wear the dress he'd bought, too.

"Can I help?" Rowan asked from the kitchen doorway. He appeared to have showered, his face freshly-shaven, his dark curls damp. He leaned against the doorjamb, half cocky, half rebellious. And completely sexy.

Louanne found it difficult not to stare, not to notice the male interest that flared in his eyes. Sexual awareness made her painfully aware of the smudge of strained peas on her white shirt and the perspiration that dampened her brow.

Was this dinner supposed to be some kind of makeshift date? Or was he just trying to be a nice guy?

It was hard to say, especially since that nice guy was making her pulse soar and her imagination spark.

He'd asked her a question, but she couldn't seem to recall what it was. Had he asked whether she needed his help?

"I've got everything under control. And I…uh… just need to get Noah ready for bed."

"I'll take him for you." Rowan slid her that bad-boy smile that sent her heart spinning like an out of control top on a hardwood floor. "So you can get dressed for dinner."

"You'll put pajamas on Noah?" Her mouth had surely dropped. Was this the same guy who balked at keeping an eye on the baby last night? "Are you sure you want to tackle something like that?"

Rowan tore his gaze from hers, settling on her son. "Do you want me to give it a shot, pal?"

Noah lurched toward Rowan, and the man took him in his arms.

"Diapering him is kind of tough," Louanne said, feeling as though she should be honest. "He squirms around quite a bit. It's like a game to him."

Rowan froze. "You want me to put on his diaper?"

The frightened look in his eyes was priceless, and she grinned. "Well, you'll have to take the old one off first."

"Change his pants?" The guy appeared to be taken aback.

Louanne couldn't hold back a laugh. "Maybe you ought to let me change his diaper, then you can lasso him and get his pajamas on."

"Good idea," Rowan said with a grin. Then he followed her into Noah's room.

Making a point of showing him how to fold a diaper, Louanne managed to get the job done in record time, in part because Noah seemed mesmerized by Rowan standing over him. She slipped a pair of rubber pants over his double diaper, noting her rapidly growing son would need a larger size soon.

Disposable diapers would probably make life a whole lot easier, but she couldn't warrant the additional expense.

She pulled a pair of summer pajamas out of Noah's bureau drawer and handed them to Rowan. "Do you think you can dress him for bed?"

"How hard can it be?"

Pretty difficult, at times, but she didn't forewarn

him. In fact, a part of her wanted to stand back, so she could watch what might prove to be an entertaining show.

"I can handle this little guy," Rowan said. "Why don't you go change your clothes?"

"It might take a while," Louanne said. "I'm not slipping into that new outfit without a shower and a shampoo."

Rowan liked the idea of her putting some effort into dressing for dinner—dressing for him. He slid her a slow, easy smile. "Take all the time you need."

She seemed to ponder the idea, then smiled and walked away, leaving Rowan alone with the baby.

He blew out a sigh, then held up the blue-and-yellow pajamas. Two pieces—top and bottom. Snaps all over the place. Why the hell did they put fasteners along the waist?

Rowan had been sleeping in the raw so long, he couldn't recall the last time he'd worn anything to bed. Another revelation.

Why the hell couldn't he remember something solid—something that would help him make sense of things?

He slipped the little shirt on the baby. That was easy enough. But before he could snap the last button, Noah rolled over and crawled to the far side of the crib at a speedy pace.

"Come back here," Rowan said with a smile. "We're not done, yet."

Noah grinned, his eyes—the same golden-brown hue as his mother's—glistened in challenge.

"So that's how it is. I've got to catch you?"

Noah shrieked.

Three minutes later, Rowan managed to corral the kid and get his pajamas on, but he didn't mess with the snaps in the waistband.

Now what?

Noah popped a thumb into his mouth, watching Rowan carefully, as if to see how much the bedtime routine had actually changed.

What was the next item on the nighty-night list? "Now I lay me down to sleep?" A story?

He wasn't sure, but he had half a notion to give the kid a hug and a kiss good-night, although he wasn't sure where that idea came from.

Instead, he gently brushed a hand across the light brown wisps of downy-soft hair. "Sleep tight, pal."

As Rowan turned toward the door, Noah blurted out a cry of protest, and Rowan wasn't sure what to do. Did he stay and try to coax the kid to sleep? Did he go and let the little guy fuss for a while?

Taking a chance, he flipped off the light switch. "It's time for bed, Noah."

Silence followed him out of the room, so he figured he'd lucked out.

Now all he had to do was get the table set up on the porch. He'd contemplated buying flowers and a candle for ambiance, while he and Pete were in town.

But when Pete had poked fun at him for picking up a bottle of chardonnay at the liquor store, he decided not to let the old man know he meant to treat Louanne to a little romance.

The flowers would have to wait until another time, but the darkened porch made candles a logical choice. He wondered whether Louanne had any stashed someplace. He supposed he'd have to look.

A couple of minutes later, he spotted a set of candlesticks on the fireplace mantel.

Had he always set a romantic mood when dining with a lady at home? It sure came easy for him. And the process had triggered some other memories, albeit nothing he'd call crucial or important. But as he'd perused the shelves at the liquor store, he'd realized he possessed a respectable knowledge of California wines. Where and how that information developed, he couldn't be sure, but there hadn't seemed to be any reason to hang a star on it.

He'd chosen a bottle of Stag's Leap chardonnay, which was now chilling in the refrigerator.

And as he prepared dinner, he wondered where he'd learned to make chicken piccata, but the proper ingredients had seemed to magically pop into his grocery cart earlier today. And his hands knew exactly what to do.

At times, he felt as though his memory was within reach, but he couldn't find the key that would open the floodgates.

Remembering things one piece at a time was frustrating.

He fumbled his way through the kitchen, discovering a knife to slice the French bread, a bowl for the salad and two goblets that didn't match. And when he'd almost given up, he found a corkscrew for the wine.

He removed the cork and carried the chilled bottle and two glasses out to the front porch.

Louanne wasn't lying when she said it would take a while, but Rowan didn't mind waiting. In fact, the anticipation of seeing her in the new dress grew steadily.

And by the time he had set the table and lit the candles, she still hadn't come out of her bedroom.

Okay, so the table and setting was a bit rustic, but he'd set a romantic mood. And even the heavens had done their part to create a star-twinkling backdrop. He hoped Louanne would appreciate his efforts, and that this evening would make her feel special.

Maybe she'd loosen up about leaving the ranch— no matter what her reasons were for remaining on the property.

Footsteps sounded down the hall, and Rowan peered through the screen door, into the living room, and spotted Louanne. She looked radiant. Stunning.

He stood on the porch like a befuddled high school freshman who'd been approached by the prom queen in full homecoming regalia.

Hell, he'd figured Louanne would look good in green, and the dress had looked great on the hanger.

But he'd never imagined how damn hot it would look on the tall, leggy brunette. In fact, if he didn't know better, he would have thought the dress had been designed for her body alone.

He shook off the initial adolescent reaction and opened the screen door to get a better view, to close the distance between them.

Wow. A scooped neckline revealed the swell of her breasts, and narrow shoulder straps adorned her shoulders and chest, showing just enough skin to make a man wonder what lay beyond the green garment. The slinky material complemented every curve of her body. And Rowan had to make a conscious effort not to gape and gawk.

A man with a pretty woman like that on his arm would want to hold her close all evening, with his hand possessively riding along the gentle contour of her hip.

"You look lovely," he said. "And whoever designed that dress would be amazed at what you've done for it."

"Thank you." A blush only made her look prettier. She'd let her long brown hair hang loose, over her shoulders. And she wore makeup—not too much, just a splash of lipstick and a dab of mascara—just enough to draw a man's attention to her eyes, the perfect cheekbones and the classic heart shape of her face.

Just enough to make a man want to draw close. To mark his territory with a hug and a kiss.

"Why don't you come outside?" he suggested. "I'll pour you a glass of wine."

She seemed to flounder a moment, as though uncomfortable with the compliment. Or maybe with the way he was looking at her. Hell, she'd have to be a fool not to see the interest in his eyes or sense his desire to kiss her again.

Rowan wasn't sure what was in the cards tonight. But he intended to let this hand play itself out.

Candlelight flickered on the patio table, competing with a silvery half-moon and a splatter of twinkling stars. The air was laden with the chirps of crickets and the songs of bullfrogs near the creek.

Dinner had been perfect. Special. Delicious. Louanne couldn't remember the last time she'd spent such a lovely evening—on the ranch or anywhere.

Rowan refilled her glass of wine, and although she wasn't really inclined to drink alcohol, the romantic ambiance made it difficult to resist.

"It's nice outside tonight," he said.

"I used to read out here on the porch. And even as darkness settled, I found it hard to drag myself out of a story long enough to go inside or turn on the porch light." Louanne fingered the stem of her wine glass and smiled at the memory. "Someone would always take pity on me, though, and flip the switch."

"You like to read?"

"I used to. When I was younger, I loved books,

particularly literature." She wasn't sure why she'd opened up. The wine maybe? Or was she becoming more comfortable with Rowan?

"Used to?" His eyes flickered in the candlelight. "You don't like to read anymore?"

"I started writing a book a couple years ago and spent my free time in front of my laptop computer. And I suppose I just haven't renewed my old reading habits."

"Did you finish the book?"

She didn't answer right away. And when she did, she told the truth. "No. I stopped writing before Noah was born."

"Why?"

What could she say? That her literary efforts, as well as her dreams and the promise of an exciting future had been dashed by a crazed man who wanted to own her body, heart and soul? A man who'd threatened to kill her if he couldn't have her to himself?

Rowan continued to stare at her, to slowly uncover every lie she'd ever told. Or at least, that's the way it felt.

"Things were different while I was in college. It was easy to dream. But I wasn't living in the real world. And when I moved home to the ranch and became a mother, reality settled in." She tried to shake off the morose millstone that her spirit lugged around and forced a smile. "Who knows? Maybe I'll find time to read again."

"And time to dream?" he asked.

How had he known that she'd given up her dreams? Did he suspect that the nightmares had taken their place?

Yet each time she caught Rowan's eye, each time she felt that spark of desire heat her blood, she felt her imagination stirring. And it seemed foolish. A complete waste of time and energy. After all, with Richard waiting to pounce on her, she couldn't very well think of love and romance or fame and fortune.

So she shrugged off his question with another. "What good does it do to dream?"

Rowan didn't know who or what had hurt Louanne. He suspected Noah's father had done a real number on her. And the loss of her parents had to have been tough. He hated the idea that her hopes— and possibly her spirit—had been squelched.

A response came to mind, a piece of advice. And like some of the other things that had leaked out of his black box of memories, he had no idea where it had come from or why it had meant something to him.

Still, he shared it with her. "Someone once told me that God didn't put a dream in one's heart without giving a person the ability to make that dream come true."

"Do you believe that?" she asked.

Yes, he did. But he wasn't sure why. He slowly nodded. "Yeah. I do believe it."

A kindred feeling settled around them, as did awareness. And attraction.

Louanne must have felt it, too, because she tore her gaze away from his, pushed her chair back, got to her feet and began to pick up the dishes. "It's getting late."

Yeah. Too late to ignore what was going on between them. Rowan stood and took the plates from her hands, replacing them on the table. Then he cupped her jaw to draw her gaze back to his, back where he wanted it.

His thumb drew slow circles on her cheek, but she didn't pull away. Didn't blink an eye. She just stood there, caught up in the heat of the moment—or so it seemed. Maybe he was the one who was lost in a battle of hormones and pheromones and lust.

But when he opened his arms, she fell into his embrace and lifted her mouth to his.

Obviously, he wasn't fighting the battle alone.

Chapter Eight

The kiss began slow and easy, like the first one they'd shared, but it quickly grew fast and reckless.

Rowan's tongue sought every moist inch of Louanne's warm, velvety mouth, as his hands slid along the slinky fabric of the dress he'd bought her. The texture heightened the sensitivity of his touch, as he caressed the slope of her back and the curve of her hips.

Passion flared, testosterone surged, and he couldn't get enough of the willing woman in his arms.

It had been ages since he'd wanted a woman this badly—if he ever had.

He wasn't sure how he knew that, but he did. And for some reason, he suspected that realization ought to scare the hell out of him, although he didn't know why.

Maybe because his blood was pumping out of control, and the kiss seemed full of promises Rowan wasn't sure either of them were ready to make. But that didn't mean he wanted to slow things down or that he wanted the woman in his arms any less.

And there was no question about it. She wanted him, too. Badly. He could tell by the way she whimpered when his hands sought her breasts, when his fingers skimmed her hardened nipples. He could tell by the way her hands stroked his body, claiming him as he claimed her.

The breath-stealing kiss intensified, stoking a fire in his blood and a hunger in his soul.

Rowan cupped her derriere and pulled her flush against the blood-pounding ache only she could relieve. Instead of balking at the strength of his arousal, she nestled against him—providing both ecstasy and agony at the same time.

A coyote howled in the distance, reminding him where they were and where they ought to be—in the comfort and privacy of a candlelit bedroom.

Should he lead her into the house and let passion carry them both away? Or stay here for a while longer, letting the magical moment build under a canopy of stars?

Before he had a chance to make a decision, Louanne gently pushed against his chest, slowing the rush and cooling the heat.

"I'm sorry." She ran a hand through the strands of her hair. "That was a crazy thing for us to do."

He wanted to argue, but what was the use? With no memories to help him wage either a defense or an agreement, he was left with lust and hormones dictating his actions, as well as his fate.

Somehow, his conscience managed to break free.

What did he have to offer her—other than a night of lovemaking that promised to be hot and fulfilling?

It certainly would be enough for him, but as a single mother trying hard to keep a ranch in the red and to raise her son, she needed more than a man who didn't know where he'd been or where he was going.

No wonder she had reservations about letting the magic play out.

Rowan wanted to be noble and understanding, yet his desire hadn't abated. If anything, he wanted her more than when their lips had been locked and their hands had sought the mysteries that lay beyond their clothing.

But taking things to a deeper level was more than a physical craving. There was a lot more hanging in the balance than sexual fulfillment. As the devil and angel on his shoulder battled it out, his words, like his memories failed him when he needed them most.

He blew out a ragged breath and raked a hand through his hair. Damn the amnesia that kept him from being whole. And damn the pull this woman had on him.

He'd had sexual relationships before—many times, it seemed. But they'd never touched him on an emotional level, never stirred his conscience. At least, he didn't think any of them had.

And right now, his emotions were running amok.

Maybe it was the amnesia causing everything to blur and tumble. That had to be it. Maybe he was on the verge of remembering things, and all the bottled up feelings were trying to bust free.

He had half a notion to kiss her again, to see if things would begin to make sense. But this was no time to play around. Louanne deserved a guy who could commit—a man with both feet on the ground and a solid game plan.

Fighting the urge to take her back into his arms, Rowan shoved his hands in his pockets. "I'm the one who should be sorry for kissing you like that. Hell, I don't even know who I am."

Louanne understood exactly how he felt. Because, when they'd kissed, when she'd lost herself in his embrace, she'd completely forgotten who she was. And, more importantly, why she shouldn't get involved with another man.

What if she made another mistake? Trusted another man who would threaten and hurt her?

More than two years ago, she'd fallen for Richard's charm, then watched him evolve into a stalker and a sociopath. He'd tried to control every aspect of their relationship, every part of her—body, heart and mind.

Rowan, of course, seemed completely different than Richard.

But he, as well as his past, were a mystery.

Did that past involve violence?

For some reason—wishful thinking, maybe—it didn't seem likely.

When she'd come to her senses in the midst of a star-spinning, knee-weakening kiss and changed her mind, Rowan had respected her decision. He hadn't seemed particularly happy about it. But he'd stopped. Stepped away.

Richard wouldn't have been that understanding. He would have grown angry. Demanding.

And she had the scars to prove it.

The black-and-blue marks he'd left on her body had faded with time. But not the bruise he'd left on her heart. And his accusations and threats still rang in her mind.

Oh, dear God. What if Richard showed up? He'd always flown into a rage when he suspected she was seeing someone else. What would happen if he actually found her romantically or sexually involved with another man—with Rowan?

The fear she'd wanted to leave behind at Cedar Glen eased back, but she forced it aside. Richard didn't know where she was. She'd hidden her tracks well. And as long as she drew no attention to herself or her whereabouts, she and Noah were safe.

She looked in Rowan's eyes, saw him waiting for

a response. Her lips were still warm and tingling from his kiss, her pulse still surging, but she forced herself to be rational.

"You don't have anything to be sorry about," she told him, before gathering the plates he'd taken from her earlier. "I made a mistake once, and I'm not ready to jump into another relationship right now."

"I understand," he said, although she doubted whether he had any idea how big a mistake her relationship with Richard had been.

Then he picked up the empty bottle of wine and, before snatching the pair of tarnished silver candlesticks that had belonged to her grandmother, he blew against the flickering flames.

Like the fiery kiss and the romantic ambiance they'd once shared, the candlelight faded to black.

For just one, brief, regret-filled moment, Louanne watched the curling wisps of smoke disappear into the night.

The Harley was more beat-up than anything. And with a little effort and a mechanical knowledge that seemed to spring from nowhere, Rowan managed to get the bike running the next afternoon.

There was, he supposed, no reason to remain on the ranch. But he had nowhere else to go at the moment. Nowhere he wanted to be. And until his memory returned, providing him options, it felt like this was a nice place to wait.

As he rolled the scraped and dented Fat Boy out of the barn and into the bright afternoon light, he spotted Louanne on her knees in the garden. From the playpen, Noah watched over his mother, as she plucked zucchini squash from a bushy vine.

They hadn't spoken about the kiss they'd shared, about the desire that brewed just under the surface— not while Rowan helped with the dishes last night, and not this morning over breakfast.

The summer breeze blew a wisp of hair from the single braid she wore. Even in a pair of faded denim overalls, she was a sight to behold.

She paused for a moment, looking over the dark green squash she'd picked, then arched and stretched her back.

The woman worked hard. Too hard, it seemed. And other than Noah and pride in a hearty garden, she didn't seem to find much pleasure in life. Just a little television in the evening and an occasional card game with Aggie and Pete.

What kind of life was that?

He glanced down at the Harley, wondering if she'd like to take a ride with him. Maybe become a carefree kid again and leave her worries behind—if only for a short while.

There was only one way to find out.

As Rowan approached the garden that lined the side of the house, Noah spotted him and let out a happy squeal.

Had anyone ever been delighted to see Rowan before? He didn't know, but it felt damn good to know the little baby liked him.

Louanne looked up and shielded her eyes from the afternoon sun with a dirt-smudged hand. "Did you get the motorcycle running?"

Rowan nodded. "I was going to take it out on a test run. Would you like to ride along?"

Interest sparked a light in her eyes, then she glanced at her son, at the garden, at her hands. "I'd better pass."

"Why?" he asked. "I'm sure Aggie can watch Noah. Besides, it will do you good to have some fun. Other than an evening playing cards, I can't think of anything you've done for pleasure."

For a moment, he considered the kiss they'd shared, the sexual pleasure it had promised. But he tossed the thought aside.

Louanne wasn't ready for their relationship to take a turn like that. And neither was he—not until his memory returned. Of course, whenever he was close enough to touch her, his libido put up a hell of an argument.

She glanced toward the small clapboard house where Aggie and Pete lived. Then she bit her bottom lip and returned her gaze to his. "If Aggie can look after Noah, maybe I'll join you for a ride."

Rowan didn't try to mask the smile that stole across his face or still the sense of excitement.

Ten minutes later, after Noah had been welcomed

into Aggie's loving arms and Louanne had gone inside, washed her hands and freshened up, she climbed on the back of the Harley. She placed her hands loosely upon his waist. "You're not going to drive too fast, are you?"

He looked over his shoulder and grinned. "I'll keep it under a hundred. Are you ready?"

She nodded, then gripped him tighter.

Rowan felt a surge of pride to have Louanne behind him, holding on. And it felt damn good to rev the engine, to accelerate and take off down the dirt drive.

Riding the Harley, he realized, had been something he'd done often. An escape he'd relished.

When they reached the county road, Rowan opened up the accelerator.

A thrill shot through Louanne, as the engine roared and the bike raced down the road, kicking up dust, racing the wind. And for the first time in what seemed like forever, her worries couldn't seem to keep up.

She didn't know how long they'd ridden, how long she'd clung to Rowan, leaving her cares behind. Not long enough, she suspected. But when they reached the fork in the road that led to Cottonwood Creek, she raised her arm and pointed out the route she wanted him to take.

He nodded, then drove to the lake that fed the meandering stream Louanne and Lula had always hiked along. He must have been impressed with the tranquil spot, too, because he eased the Harley to a halt near a field of wildflowers and cut the engine.

A lonely whippoorwill called in the trees, where dappled sunlight spotted the ground. Louanne climbed from the bike, and Rowan followed her lead. She paused along the shady shoreline, enjoying the natural beauty, the warmth of the sun, the earthy scent, the twitter of birds in the trees.

A sense of expectation settled around her as Rowan took her hand in his. She ought to pull away, but she threaded her fingers through his instead, wanting this moment to last.

Whether it was the lingering endorphins from the exhilarating ride that had momentarily freed her soul, the natural beauty of the Texas country-side, the attractive man who set her heart on end or a powerful combination of all three, she couldn't be sure.

But either way, when Rowan turned and caught her eye, desire flared and her common sense bit the dust. As though having a mind of its own, her hand wrapped around his neck, and she pulled his mouth to hers.

Their hands and lips seemed to know exactly where they'd left off, and the kiss grew hungry, but controlled—as though they were lovers who had all the time in the world to explore, to caress, to plea-sure each other over and over again.

The kiss was magical, as well as arousing. And

Louanne lost herself in Rowan's embrace, in his musky scent, in his tantalizing taste.

Had she ever wanted to throw caution to the wind before? Let her passion rule her mind and her heart? Make love in the grass with a devilishly good-looking man who had the eyes of an angel and an arousing touch that drove her wild?

But all good things came to an end, or at least they did in Louanne's life.

This time, Rowan was the one to break the connection. He caught her jaw in his hand, circled a thumb on her cheek, snagged her attention with a sky-blue gaze that was clouded with heat and desire.

There was nothing Rowan wanted more than to lay Louanne down in a field of grass and make love to her in the light of day. He knew where the kiss had been heading, where their thoughts had drifted. Where their shared desire would lead. And he remembered what she'd said last night.

Had she changed her mind? Was she now willing to complicate their relationship? Risk taking things to a deeper, more committed level?

It wasn't just her own life she had to think about. She was a mother. And every decision she made would affect the life of her child.

"Are you sure about this?" he asked, giving her an out, yet hoping she wouldn't take it.

"I'm sure about wanting to make love with you more than I've ever wanted anyone before." Her eyes sought his, conveying a silent reluctance, as she bit down on her bottom lip. "But it still isn't right. And I'm afraid it might never be."

Rowan nodded, then drew away. His arms hung loosely at his sides. Empty. But what else was new? His mind had been empty for days.

"Thank you for understanding."

He supposed that called for a "you're welcome," but the words wouldn't form. He didn't feel particularly gracious, so he didn't deserve her thanks. Instead, he smiled wryly. "My memory is still out of my reach, but I have a feeling being noble and understanding isn't in my nature."

"Maybe not, but you have no idea how much I appreciate the fact that you're honoring my reluctance." She brushed a light kiss upon his cheek. "Are you ready to go?"

No, he wasn't. He wanted to stay out here in the Texas countryside, making love until the sun set. But he nodded in acquiescence.

Then she turned toward the parked motorcycle, putting an end to their wild escape from reality.

A baby cried, filling the darkened bedroom and jerking Rowan from a sound sleep.

Noah.

Was something wrong? Where was Louanne? Hadn't she heard the little guy?

Rowan threw off the covers, climbed from bed and

slipped into a pair of pants. Then he followed the cries to the living room, where Louanne, her hair tousled from sleep, held the fussing baby in her arms, rocking back and forth on the sofa.

"What's the matter?" he asked, feeling helpless.

"His tooth is bothering him." Louanne continued her movements. "I'm sorry we woke you."

"Don't be." He raked a hand through his hair and studied the pretty mother in a worn cotton gown, finding himself even more drawn to her, more attracted. And interestingly enough, seeing her maternal side only seemed to deepen her appeal.

How did she know what was bothering Noah? The kid couldn't talk. Maybe his stomach hurt. Or he'd had a bad dream.

"What makes you think that he has a toothache?" Rowan asked.

Louanne smiled as though she'd gotten the punch line of a joke and he hadn't. "That's not it. He's teething. And I can tell it hurts because the gums are red and puffy on the bottom left side."

That made sense. He realized there was a lot he didn't know about babies. What kind of a dad would he make, if he couldn't figure out what end of a baby was up?

But then again, maybe Noah's own father wouldn't have been any better at this stuff than Rowan was.

The baby nestled against his mother's breast, his

cries easing some. At times like this, Louanne must miss not having a man around to share the parental load.

"Do you ever wish Noah's dad was around to help out?" Rowan asked.

The motherly expression froze, and she lifted her gaze from the baby boy in her arms. "No. I don't. He's not a nice man. And he wouldn't have made a good husband or a father."

Then why had she slept with him? Why had she risked having a child with a man like that? "You must have seen something decent in him."

"At first, yes." She placed a comforting hand lightly against the child's head, against his ear, as though shielding him from her words. "But it wasn't long before he let me see the real man behind the facade."

Rowan was unwilling to let the subject die, although he wasn't entirely sure why. "And you got pregnant before you could end things?"

"To make a long story short, that's about the size of it." She tore her gaze from his, focusing on the fretful child. But he sensed it was her way of ending an uncomfortable conversation.

A minute or two later, as Louanne rocked back and forth, Noah grew quiet, his head still resting against his mother's heart. His eyes fluttered momentarily, then closed.

It had to be uncomfortable for her to sway like that, her back not supported.

Rowan lowered his voice, so as not to disturb the child. "You need a rocking chair."

"I had one," she whispered softly. "But the darned old thing is so ancient, it gave out one evening, and I nearly fell on the floor."

"Is it an antique?"

"I was told my great-great-grandmother brought it to Texas by covered wagon in the late 1800s, and it was a family heirloom then. So, I guess it just wore out from overuse."

Rowan couldn't quell a mounting curiosity. "Where is it?"

She nodded toward the hall. "In Noah's closet. I was going to haul it out to the barn, but I haven't gotten around to it yet."

An overwhelming urge to see the antique and study the workmanship caused Rowan to excuse himself and go in search of the rocker. He entered Noah's bedroom, opened the closet door and pulled out the broken chair.

He could see why Louanne thought it was useless, but looking beyond the varnish that had been darkened and cracked by age, Rowan marveled at the hand-crafted spindles, the solid mahogany wood.

The rocker needed to be repaired, but the quality of the wood and the skill of the craftsman couldn't be replicated today, other than by another master carpenter who loved his work.

And Rowan was that master carpenter. He wasn't exactly sure how he knew. But he did.

He could repair the antique rocking chair. And properly, too.

As he stroked the wood, the carved headrest, his memory reeled and a hodgepodge of images flashed before him. They shuffled like a deck of cards, as his mind tried to sort through the jumbled mess.

A bar fight. A chair slammed against the wall. A fist to the jaw. Another drunk dragging him out the door. Sirens blaring. A midnight run to safety.

Poker games that lasted until dawn. Afternoons in a carpentry shop built over a garage.

A sense of grief settled around Rowan, the same grief that had been haunting him since he regained consciousness. It blindsided him with a solemn grave-side service, a military chaplain with a worn leather bible in hand, a recorded twenty-one-gun-salute.

He wasn't sure how long he stood there like that, his mind going a hundred miles an hour and producing only bits and pieces of memory to grab hold of. He felt like a drowning man reaching for debris rushing along in the rage of a flooded river.

There was so much to remember, so much still hidden. He didn't have a grasp of everything, but something useful had finally dawned.

Rowan was a master carpenter. And he'd just buried the only friend he'd ever had—a fifty-year-old alcoholic with a pragmatic view of life. His best friend, his mentor.

At a cemetery, he'd stared at the flag-draped, solid

mahogany casket with gold-plated handles and listened to a uniformed chaplain recite scripture meant to make him feel better. It hadn't.

Neither had a dark-suited, doleful representative of the funeral home, or the color guard or the tape-recorded twenty-one-gun salute. With tears blurring his vision, Rowan had stood alone at the graveside. Or at least it felt that way.

He'd lost the only thing in the world that mattered to him. The only one who really cared a damn about him.

The coroner had called it an accident caused by driving while intoxicated. But Rowan hadn't believed it. A drunken Sam Vargas hadn't lost control of his pickup and driven off the mountain road to his death. He'd stepped on the gas and turned off intentionally.

Rowan had always feared the old man's pain would grow too strong, that Rowan's friendship wouldn't be enough to keep Sam from ending the misery of a broken heart that refused to mend.

"Are you okay?" Louanne asked from the doorway, a sleeping Noah in her arms.

No, he wasn't okay. Things were a jumbled up mess. But the darkness had cleared, leaving him a clutter of memories to clean up and sort through.

Somehow, he managed to nod, while he scooped up the two pieces of the rocker and carried them into the living room.

He had a feeling Louanne would follow him, after

she put Noah back to bed. She'd looked at him with knowing eyes, as though aware of his struggle to remember and willing to help him sort through his thoughts.

But sharing his feelings wasn't something that came easy to Rowan.

And now that Sam had died, he wasn't sure whether he would ever open up again.

Chapter Nine

"What happened in there?" Louanne, no longer holding the sleeping baby, joined Rowan in the living room, where he stood over the rocking chair that had triggered his memory.

He didn't respond, in part because he was just beginning to grasp what had happened himself. But there was another reason he held his tongue. Rowan wasn't used to putting his feelings into words.

"You appeared to be deep in thought." She eased closer. "I hope that means you're beginning to remember things."

A tear welled in Rowan's eye, and he swiped it aside with the back of his hand in a desperate attempt to hide his emotion. He turned his head, avoiding her gaze.

But she didn't take the hint. "Do you want to talk about it?"

No. Yes. Hell, he didn't know. But maybe if he voiced his scattered thoughts, the pictures would fall into place and revelations of Sam would unleash the rest of his memories. He just hoped the other images locked away in his mind weren't as unsettling as this one.

Louanne took his hand and gave it a squeeze. "I can sit with you, or leave you alone—whichever will make you feel better."

He gripped her hand tightly, not wanting her to leave, yet reluctant to share the mishmash of feelings with anyone, especially her.

Yet maybe she was right. Talking it out might help. But where did he start? Which memory did he call up?

The funeral was the most recent.

The bar fight came first.

He closed his eyes and tried to clear a vision of the night he'd first met Sam.

It had been late—a hot, dry and windy Saturday night in late September. A Santa Ana condition, Southern Californians called it.

A frat house party was just beginning to pick up steam, but Rowan had grown restless; he didn't know why. The heat? A fight with his old man? Maybe both.

So he'd thumbed his way from Westwood to the

Sunset Strip, where he found the nightlife more interesting. More entertaining.

Being underage had never stopped Rowan from drinking or bellying up to a bar. He'd matured earlier than most teenage boys. As long as he was being served by a woman, he'd merely had to flash a smile rather than the fake ID he kept in his pocket. And that night at Wild Willie's had been no different.

"I met Sam Vargas in a bar. He was a fifty-year-old drunk who was getting his butt kicked by a couple of beefy bouncers." Rowan shrugged. "Things are still a little disjointed. But for some reason, I have an idea I'd been warned to stay out of nightclubs and keep my nose clean, but I wasn't much for heeding rules."

"Sam must have been pretty special," she said. "You had his number programmed in the top position of your cell phone directory."

Rowan nodded. "He was. I didn't know it at the time, but that surly old alcoholic would become the best friend I ever had."

She smiled, as though understanding something that was just making sense to him. "What did you do? Help Sam find his way home and tend his wounds?"

Rowan slid her a cocky grin. "No, actually, he took me home and tended mine."

She lifted a brow. "I thought Sam was getting the butt-kicking."

"Yeah, but I couldn't just stand by and watch."

Rowan shrugged. "I've always been pretty scrappy, I guess. And two big, sober thugs beating on a skinny old drunk didn't seem fair to me. So I figured I'd even the match."

"Did you?"

"In a way." An odd sense of pride settled over him. "The bartender called the police, and I knew I'd be in a ton of trouble if they figured out the ID I carried was fake. And Sam would probably get hauled to jail. So we took off like two drunks in a three-legged gunnysack race, staggering, falling down, helping each other get up again and laughing like hell."

"This is getting more interesting than a good novel. What happened next?"

"Sam took me home to his house in Hollywood Hills, and after celebrating our bravery, washing the blood from our faces and our scraped knuckles, I crashed on his sofa. And the next morning, he showed me his workshop." Rowan relived the moment, the bond that the late-night brawl had forged. And he thanked his lucky stars that he'd gotten to know the older man, because the two barroom buddies developed a friendship that gave Rowan a purpose in life—even if that purpose hadn't been enough to give Sam a reason to keep living.

"What kind of workshop did Sam have?" she asked.

"He was a master carpenter. And he'd made a fortune at his craft, but his wife died four years ago, leaving him wasted by grief. The nights were the hardest for him, so each evening he did his best to drown his sorrow in 90 proof."

Rowan found more than a friend and a father figure in Sam. He found a mentor, as well as a craft he loved. So he overlooked Sam's fondness for Jack Daniel's whiskey—straight up—and soaked up every woodworking lesson and each piece of advice the pragmatic old carpenter shared.

In hindsight, Rowan probably should have directed Sam to an AA meeting, but at the time, he was drowning a few of his own sorrows. He wasn't sure why, though. That part of his memory was still locked away.

"Sam's phone number had been disconnected," Louanne said, her voice soft and gentle, as though trying to nudge his memory.

But it wasn't necessary. "Sam died a couple of weeks ago, after he missed a turn on a winding mountain grade, crashed through a guardrail and went over the edge."

"I'm sorry."

"Me too. Sam was the father I never really had." Rowan furrowed his brow and closed his eyes, trying to block out the memory he'd temporarily forgotten. But it wasn't any use. His grief wouldn't let the truth slip away. "The police report said he'd been drinking, which was true. And they chalked it up as another drunk driving statistic. But I don't think that's exactly what happened."

"You don't think alcohol played a part in the accident?"

"Oh, it contributed to a degree. Sometimes drinking helped Sam forget. But other times, it made him more melancholy. More depressed." Rowan looked up and caught her sympathetic gaze. "You know what I think?"

"What?"

"I think he wanted to end it all and join his wife."

She nodded, as though understanding. But what he didn't tell her, what he would keep inside until his dying day, was that he hadn't been there for his friend that night.

Another tear escaped, slipping down Rowan's face, and he quickly swiped it away. But not before Louanne spotted it.

He wanted to hide his pain, retreat into a world of his own, which he suspected was his natural reaction to painful emotions.

But she wouldn't let him. She slipped her arms around him, offering the same loving embrace she'd recently offered her teary-eyed son.

He should have waved her off, sucked it up. Told her he wasn't a baby. Insisted it was only one little tear, and that he had everything under control.

Instead, he rested his head against her cheek, closed his eyes, lost himself in her breezy, wildflower scent and accepted whatever she had to offer.

It helped, he supposed. The comfort. The understanding. But it also stirred something else—something much bigger than a growing arousal and an overwhelming desire to take her to bed.

It stirred the kind of things that were best left alone—soft and sappy things that made a guy weak and vulnerable. Made him want to say all kinds of things he couldn't possibly mean.

Rowan wasn't sure where all the emotional stuff was coming from.

The lust he could deal with—the urge to make love with Louanne, then go on his way. But what he found more unsettling was the desire to stay wrapped in her arms for as long as she would hold him.

And that scared the hell out of him.

He slowly pulled away, then dragged a hand through his hair. "I…umm… I'm sorry for running off at the mouth like that. And for being such a wussy."

"Hurting from the loss of a friend isn't something to be ashamed of."

No. But letting someone know how torn up he was inside didn't sit well with him. "Yeah, well, thanks for listening."

"Anytime."

He nodded, then walked away, down the hall and into his bedroom. Once inside, he closed the door—but only on Louanne. Not on the feelings and urges she'd aroused. He slipped off his pants and climbed back into bed. But he couldn't sleep. Way too much had happened tonight.

Yet there was still a lot more to deal with—his anger and resentment for one, especially since he didn't seem to have a target for it.

Something told him the painful memory of Sam was only the tip of the iceberg.

And he doubted whether Louanne's soothing embrace would help defuse the raw emotions that still simmered somewhere in the murky depths of his mind.

The night passed slowly and fretfully, as Louanne tossed and turned. In spite of her exhaustion, her mind and heart refused to rest.

She'd tried to comfort Rowan in his grief, but couldn't have been much help. The man had pulled away and returned to his room, broad shoulders carrying a load she couldn't share.

According to Rowan, Sam became the dad he never really had. And his sister Emily said Rowan had never gotten along with their father.

Did Louanne dare call Emily again? Dig into Rowan's past so she could shed some light on things?

Not without Rowan's okay. It wouldn't be right, no matter how badly she wanted to help, no matter how much she wanted him to find peace and renew a relationship with his father—something she'd never be able to do with hers.

She'd tried to tell herself that Rowan's problems weren't her own. That she had plenty to keep her mind active, alert, on edge. And she certainly didn't need to borrow more worries. But it didn't seem to help.

Finally, an hour of so before dawn, her eyes grew heavy, and she eventually dozed off. When she woke, feeling tired and sluggish, she climbed from bed, peered through the blinds and realized morning had begun without her.

Louanne padded down the hall to check on Noah, who was still sound asleep, thank goodness. The poor baby boy wasn't likely to get a full night's sleep until that pesky tooth broke free.

Glad to have a bit of time to herself, in spite of it being nearly eight o'clock, she quickly showered and dressed. On her way to start breakfast, she glanced into Rowan's bedroom. Funny, how it no longer seemed like Lula's room, even with those old movie posters she'd left adorning the walls.

The door was open, the bed made.

Obviously, Rowan was awake. She expected to see him in the kitchen, but found it empty, with everything just as she'd left it the night before.

Where had he gone?

She wandered into the living room.

No Rowan.

And no rocking chair. Had he carried it out to the barn, as a favor to her?

She took another quick peek at Noah, found him still asleep and went outside to look for Rowan. The summer sun had made a good start on its westerly trek across the Texas sky, having already burned off the morning dew and warmed the summer breeze.

When Louanne reached the barn, she swung open the door. The whiny creak and groan of the rusty hinge reminded her it needed oil. As she stepped inside, the familiar scent of leather and hay accosted her, as tiny specks of dust and straw danced in the light of day. In the far corner near the back door, the rocking chair rested in two pieces on the worktable.

But that wasn't what caused her heart to thump or what made her catch her breath.

The Harley was gone, which meant Rowan had left. And he hadn't even said goodbye.

She knew the time was coming, that Rowan would leave someday, but she wasn't prepared for it today.

Nor was she ready for the fist of disappointment that slammed into her chest.

The Harley ran a little sluggish, but it felt good to open the throttle and race down the road. Rowan hadn't been able to sleep last night—not after opening up and dumping his grief on Louanne. So he'd risen at dawn and taken the rocking chair out to the barn, a dilapidated old building that could use some refurbishing itself.

Four dirty windows, one at each side of the structure, had provided light for his search for tools he could use. Apparently, Louanne's dad hadn't done much carpentry, so Rowan had made a mental list of what he'd need to not only fix the rocker, but restore it to mint condition.

He loved working with wood, cutting and sanding and carefully joining the pieces together in such a way that it brought out the beauty of the grain.

At one time, before Sam died, Rowan had dreamed of going into business with his mentor. But widowed and in his fifties, Sam no longer had the drive he once did, before his wife passed away.

"I lost the magic when I buried my Jenny," he'd said on several occasions.

Rowan had never fully understood the depth of his old friend's grief. Not until Sam died, leaving Rowan to suffer his own heart-wrenching loss.

The blow of Sam's death had been staggering. At first, Rowan had believed the phone call had been a mistake, that it had been someone else driving Sam's truck, another body that lay crumpled and bloody in the twisted wreckage. Then he'd gotten mad—at God, at himself. At Sam. But as reality set in, Rowan broke down and cried like a baby, something he hadn't done since second grade.

With only a bottle of Jack Daniel's—Sam's escape of choice—to keep him company, Rowan grieved that first afternoon and evening alone. But the next morning, when he'd rolled out of bed with a brutal headache and bloodshot eyes, the grief returned full throttle, threatening to take the wind out of his sails and the magic out of his dreams—just as it had done to Sam. So he'd steered clear of whiskey from that day on and tried to live with the godawful ache in his chest.

One of those hotdog celebrity shrinks on TV said grieving was a process and suggested it would run its course. Rowan just hoped to hell it would hurry up.

He slowed the Harley near the copse of cottonwoods and searched the road ahead, looking for the turn that would take him to town. There it was.

Once on the main drag, Rowan stopped at the Bluebonnet Café, where he sat at the counter and ordered biscuits and gravy, biding his time until the hardware store opened for business.

"More coffee?" A pleasant-faced, heavyset waitress in a pink-and-white dress asked.

Rowan looked at his wristwatch, then offered the middle-aged woman a smile. "Sure, why not?"

"You're new around here," she said, as she refilled his white mug. "My name is Carol Ann Dressler. What's yours?"

"Rowan Parks." The name came easy now. Yet the early years and the family ties were still a blur— clearing, he supposed, but still obscure.

"You just passing through?" the waitress asked.

He supposed so; he just hadn't felt like leaving town yet. "I'm staying out at the Lazy B Ranch."

"With Pete and Aggie?" Carol Ann slid him a broad smile and leaned a well-rounded hip against the counter. "I've lived in Pebble Creek my whole life. And I know everyone."

Rowan had a feeling the talkative waitress made it a habit of knowing everyone's personal business, too. But what the heck. Small towns and country folk were like that, he supposed, just looking out for everyone. "Yes, I'm staying with Pete and Aggie. Louanne and the baby, too."

"Louanne Brown?" the waitress lifted a makeup-enhanced brow. "I didn't know she'd come back home. Or that she'd had a baby."

That was odd. Rowan could have sworn Louanne had been working the ranch since Noah's birth. Maybe even longer than that. Her return was obviously a surprise to people in Pebble Creek. So he held his tongue. Louanne probably valued privacy as much as he did.

"Did she have a little boy or girl?" the waitress asked.

He didn't want to answer, but couldn't figure out how to get around it. "A little boy."

"That's so nice. I'll bet the Browns would have loved having a grandbaby. It's a shame they'll never get to see him." Carol Ann set the coffeepot back on the warmer. "I was hoping one of the girls would come home. But they both had such mind-boggling dreams, wanting bright lights and fame, which was certainly more than a small town like Pebble Creek could give them."

An uneasy feeling settled over Rowan, as though he'd shared a big family secret with a stranger.

Pete and Aggie mentioned that Louanne wouldn't leave the ranch.

Was she too busy? Not interested in small town life? Hiding out for a reason? Or was she, as Aggie suspected, plagued by anxiety?

Rowan didn't know, but he thought it best to let the conversation drop. He took a sip of coffee, then glanced at his watch. Not quite nine o'clock. But close enough.

"Looks like the hardware store should be open." He placed a ten-dollar bill on the counter. "Thanks, Carol Ann."

"You're more than welcome. Be sure and give Louanne my best."

He nodded. "I'll do that."

As Rowan headed toward the door, Carol Ann called out, "And tell Louanne to come into town. Folks would love to see her. The baby, too."

Twenty minutes later, after purchasing what he needed to fix the rocking chair, Rowan climbed on his Harley and rode home.

Well, not home, but back to the ranch.

God only knew where *his* home was. The address on his driver's license was a post office box in Napa—in the wine country.

When he pulled into the yard and shut off the engine, everything was quiet. He figured Louanne had taken Noah to Aggie's house, then joined Pete at work. So he got busy and repaired the rocker. Of course, refurbishing the well-made antique would take a while. But he'd do that after Noah's tooth quit bothering him, after Louanne no longer needed to rock the little guy to sleep.

He carried the rocking chair into the house, but wasn't sure where it belonged. The living room looked kind of full.

Noah's bedroom maybe?

As he headed for the baby's room, footsteps sounded on the porch, and the front door squeaked open. Damn, but the hinges in the place needed a good oiling. In fact, the run-down ranch could keep a hyperactive handyman busy for years.

"Rowan?" Louanne called from the living room.

"I'm in Noah's room."

What was he doing in there? Louanne followed his voice, unable to still the rapid beat of her heart. When she'd spotted that battered Harley parked in the yard, a huge sense of relief washed over her. Just knowing Rowan was back brought on a rush of excitement.

She'd thought he left for good.

As she entered Noah's room, Rowan stood over the rocker. It was all in one piece.

He smiled, his face lighting up when she entered the room. As he nodded toward the chair, his summer-sky eyes danced with pride. "Almost good as new."

"You fixed it?"

"Well, you can't sit in it yet. But give it a day or two and it should work as good as new."

"Thanks." His gaze lingered on her, and she lifted a hand and touched her hair in a nervous gesture, hoping he wasn't aware of how self-conscious she felt. How vulnerable.

"As soon as Noah's tooth quits bothering him, and you don't need to rock him in the middle of the night, I'd like to refurbish the chair for you. If that's okay."

"Sure. That's fine." She tried to hide her wide-eyed surprise, her relief that he meant to stay a while longer. That he'd taken time to fix the chair and wanted to actually refurbish the antique.

"I didn't know where to put it." He scanned Noah's room, then nodded toward the open closet door. "You'd stored it in there, so I figured you might want it in this room."

She nodded, amazed by his thoughtfulness. And more than just a bit swept away by the boyish look on such a devilishly handsome face. The single diamond in his ear entranced her, as did the scruffy black locks of his hair.

It didn't appear as though he found much use for a comb. Yet it didn't seem to matter. A rebellious hairstyle suited him and nearly hid the stitches Doc would remove tomorrow.

"Hey," he said, nodding toward the top shelf of the closet. "Is that a laptop?"

Her gaze followed his to the spot where she'd

placed the portable computer at the top of Noah's closet so she wouldn't have to look at it every day, wouldn't have to remember the dream she once had. "Yes, that's what it is."

"What's it doing up there?"

She shrugged her shoulders. "I don't have much use for it anymore."

"Not even for writing your novel?"

The story she was creating? For a moment, she couldn't remember where she'd left off or what conflict faced her protagonist. "I don't have time to write."

A look of skepticism settled on his face, suggesting he wasn't buying her explanation. "What if I watch Noah for you in the evenings? Or in the mornings?"

She didn't respond right away. His offer and his suggestion had triggered something deep in her heart.

Did she dare dream again?

Rowan removed the laptop from the shelf, then flashed her a smile. "Maybe, if it's out in the open for a while, you'll feel the magic again."

"The magic?" she asked.

"That's what Sam used to say. There's magic in a dream, especially when you're making it come true. I felt it when I was working with that rocking chair. And I suspect you felt it when you were writing."

She had. Would the magic return? Could a person will it to appear? Or had Louanne wasted the small portion that had been granted her?

Her skeptical side wanted to disregard what he'd said, but something powerful urged her to take hold of his words and believe again.

"Do you think we're each given just so much magic in a lifetime?" she asked, daring him to tell her the supply was unlimited.

"I don't know. But there's just one way to find out."

She knew what he meant. The source might be infinite, but she had to dig for the magic again.

Rowan took her by the hand. "Come on, let's get this thing set up."

"You don't take no for an answer, do you?"

He merely blessed her with a rebellious grin.

Rowan had repaired the rocker. And now he was touching her heart. Encouraging her to reach for the magic, whatever was left.

The biker with unruly dark hair, heavenly eyes and a bad-boy grin apparently had a knack with antique rockers.

Did he have the power to refurbish her heart and set her dreams in motion again?

Chapter Ten

The laptop sat on the scarred maple table in the dining room for nearly a week, just exactly where Rowan had left it.

But that didn't mean Louanne didn't look at it often and think about trying her hand at writing again. Especially when the compact computer sat across from her at dinner, like an uninvited guest.

When she stood to gather the used plates and flatware, Rowan stopped her. "Noah and I will do the dishes, if you feel like puttering around in here for a while."

Louanne knew what he meant. And she appreciated his offer. But sitting in front of the computer seemed fruitless.

Before, when she'd been elbow-deep in the manuscript and caught up in the story, she could have sat down at any time of the day or night and slipped right into whatever scene she'd been writing. The characters had constantly called to her. But she no longer heard them, no longer felt that same compulsion, that same drive.

Would her muse return if she booted up the computer and stared at the screen?

She looked at Rowan, spotted the crooked, boyish grin, the glimmer in his sky-blue eyes. How could she tell him no? "It will probably be a waste of time, but if you want to do the dishes and watch Noah for a while, I'll give it a try."

"Hey, buddy," Rowan said to the baby in the high chair. "You and I have KP duty. And if you're a good helper, we can hang out in the living room and play ball."

Noah grinned, his eyes lighting up as though he'd actually understood the deal.

As Rowan started to remove the baby from the high chair, he scrunched his face and looked at Louanne. "Noah sure gets messy when he eats."

"Do you want me to give him his bath first?"

Rowan paused, as though considering her offer, as though wanting to hand off the baton. But he gave a tough-guy shrug. "Heck, how hard can it be?"

Pretty hard for a man not used to babies, but she decided to let him give it his best shot. The idea of sitting in front of the keyboard didn't seem nearly as daunting as it had before.

So, while Rowan and Noah disappeared into the bathroom down the hall, Louanne pulled up a chair and sat down, her posture straight and formal, her fingers stiff and awkward. She opened the file of the work she'd saved, reading from the screen.

A while later—she didn't have any idea how long—Rowan's voice called out from the living room, "Atta boy, Noah. Gimme five. You scored a field goal! That's three points."

The baby shrieked in delight, and Rowan laughed. It was a soothing sound, a heartwarming sound.

Louanne wasn't sure what was going on in there, but it sounded like a game of baby football, which wasn't the way she played with her son. She and Noah usually looked at picture books and played peekaboo. Was rough-and-tumble activity a father's contribution to a son's childhood? Male bonding and an introduction to sports?

The smile on her face came naturally, as her heart fluttered and soared. Is that what life would be like, if Noah had a daddy living in the house?

Don't even go there, she admonished herself. Your life—and Rowans's, too—are shadowed by uncertainty of the past, as well as the future.

She tried to focus on the manuscript that had once been a work in progress, willing herself to concentrate, to read, to be drawn into the plot, to fall into that subconscious flow. To sit back and let the magic take wing.

The antique clock on the maple hutch tick-tock-ticked a steady cadence, but time gradually suspended, reality drifted away and Louanne returned to the fictitious world only she could see.

She had no idea how long she'd sat there, how much time had passed before she began to peck out the first awkward words. But slowly, the characters came back to life, playing out on the stage in her mind. And amazingly, during the long intermission, they hadn't forgotten their lines. Her fingers grew nimble, dancing upon the keyboard, picking up the story and taking it forward.

Before, while Richard was still a very real and frightening part of her life, her writing had taken on a dark tone until the words failed to come at all. But now the black veil slowly lifted, revealing the magic, as well as the dream she'd once thought had died.

If she used a pen name—not Lanay Landers, but something different, something Richard wouldn't recognize—she'd be free to submit her manuscripts for publication and not fear him finding her through some online bookstore or the computerized card catalog system in the college library.

Noah's pain-filled cry sounded from the living room, jerking Louanne back to reality. She nearly knocked over her chair as she rushed to her baby. Had the football game become too rough?

When she entered the room, Rowan held a scream-
ing Noah to his chest, rocking in comfort. His eyes
begged her forgiveness. "I'm sorry. It was all my fault."

Louanne took Noah into her arms, spotting a
bruised knot that had quickly formed on his little
forehead. She headed to the kitchen for ice. Surely
Rowan hadn't tackled the baby. "What happened?"

Rowan followed behind. "I couldn't get to him in
time. He tottered when he walked to the chair, then
he fell against the coffee table."

Louanne reached into the freezer, snagged an ice
cube, then prepared a compress to place against the
knot. Noah cried more at the administering of first
aid, than he had at the bump on his noggin.

She thought about what Rowan had said. "Noah
walked?"

He nodded. "Yeah. His all-time record is eleven
steps without falling. And he was getting braver, too.
But that last time, he took off when I wasn't looking."

Many babies walked before their first birthdays,
but for some reason, Noah had been more cautious,
taking only one or two steps away from whatever he
held on to.

Was his caution due to having an overly protective mother? Or his containment in the playpen Louanne had to rely on while she worked around the
house and in the yard?

Either way, she was glad to see her small son trying, even if Rowan was the first to witness his efforts.

"Accidents happen," she said. "This isn't the first bump Noah's had, and it certainly won't be the last."

Rowan looked at her as though he'd done something dastardly. "I feel awful."

While Louanne balanced Noah on her hip, she placed a hand on Rowan's cheek, felt the light bristle of his beard, the tingle of warmth upon contact, the invisible connection. The outpouring of thoughts and emotions she didn't understand.

He gripped her wrist, holding her palm against his face, as if he meant to hang on to the connection for fear they'd lose it.

When Noah's cries stopped, Rowan released his hold, allowing Louanne to withdraw her hand. But the connection remained. Their feelings for each other—lust, attraction or whatever—were just as powerful as they'd ever been. Maybe more so.

But the baby stood between them.

Or more likely, the child's father stood between them.

She studied Noah carefully, then looked at Rowan. "He's going to be fine."

Louanne just hoped *she* would fare as well.

Denying what she felt for Rowan, the desire and attraction she couldn't let progress naturally, was difficult to deal with, impossible to ignore.

They'd fallen into pseudo-marital roles, like mommy and daddy. But it wasn't enough. Not when sexual desire hovered around them, letting them both know exactly what their relationship was missing.

She carried Noah back into the living room, and the baby lurched forward, wanting to be placed upon the floor. When she set him down near the coffee table, he used it to pull himself up and walk around the edge as though he'd never fallen down.

Brave little guy. And determined, too. He wouldn't let fear of a tumble hold him back.

Louanne glanced at Rowan, only to find him staring at the coffee table, his eyes drilling right through the wood.

He was drifting away, like he had in Noah's bedroom, when he found the broken rocker.

She watched him, suspecting he was sorting through the memories again.

The memory struck hard and without warning, slapping against Rowan's head, throwing his six-year-old body against the glass-topped table in his father's home office.

Get the hell out of here. Can't you see I'm busy?

Rowan hadn't meant to anger his father, only to show him a picture he'd drawn.

Damn it. Walter Parks jumped up from the desk and grabbed Rowan by the arm. *Brenda, hurry up and get in here! This kid is getting blood on the carpet.*

Brenda Wheeler, the housekeeper and nanny, came running. She lifted the edge of her apron and pressed it against the side of Rowan's head. *Oh, dear. Sweetheart, what happened?*

Rowan had looked at his dad, waiting for Walter to explain that he'd batted him away—hard—without thought of the consequences.

Walter stiffened. *Can't you see I'm busy, boy? I don't have time to look at crayon chicken scratches.* Then he handed Rowan the colorful picture, the gift a small boy had offered his daddy in hopes of being accepted, appreciated. Loved.

Rowan pulled away from Brenda's embrace, crumpled up the picture and dropped it on the office floor. Then he turned his back on his father and walked away.

It was the very last time he'd cried in front of his old man—in front of anyone, for that matter. And it had been the very last time he'd tried to approach his father like a son.

Walter may have left a red, giant-sized handprint on the side of Rowan's face, as well as a scar over his left eye. But he'd left a bigger, more painful and longer lasting mark on his son's heart that rainy afternoon.

Rowan supposed his surly attitude had developed that day, as well. Or maybe that's when it had reared its head. More than likely, his badass, who-gives-a-damn attitude had been developing ever since his father had his mother locked away.

Louanne placed a gentle hand on his forearm. "Are you okay?"

Yeah, he was okay, even though he was drowning in memories that had come flooding back, memories he wished had never returned. "Don't worry about me. I'll be all right."

And he would be.

Rowan no longer gave a squat about being loved or accepted by his old man. He didn't need Walter Parks, the jewelry empire the man had built or the damn fortune he'd accumulated.

In fact, Rowan didn't need anyone or anything.

After watching Noah for a while and deciding he hadn't suffered any more than a black-and-blue knot on his head, Louanne put the baby to bed. Then she returned to the living room, only to find Rowan on the porch.

He stood against the railing, looking into the night. He'd told her he was okay. But she didn't believe him.

"Want to talk about it?" she asked.

He turned slowly and shrugged. "I don't see any point in stirring up stuff I've been trying to forget for years."

Louanne sensed Rowan's anger had to do with the man he'd never gotten along with. And she suspected he'd feel better if he talked about it. "It's your father, isn't it?"

Rowan nodded. "Yeah. That's what's bothering me. That's where the anger comes from. My dad never gave a damn about me. He was too caught up in his jewelry mining business to care about any of the kids, particularly one who looked like the wife he had committed to a hospital in Switzerland."

A thousand thoughts swirled in Louanne's mind. The first being Rowan's mention of jewelry. Rowan was part of *that* Parks family? They had to be worth a king's fortune and certainly way out of her league. But the second and more unsettling thought was the fact that he'd grown up without a mother.

"I'm sorry to hear about your mom."

His tortured soul peered out of his gaze, touching something in her heart. "My older brother and sister—the twins, Cade and Emily—remember her. But I don't. So I can't say that I missed her."

She supposed he meant to downplay his loss. But she didn't buy it. "It must have been tough for you anyway."

He nodded. "I guess so. For the most part, we were raised by the housekeeper, Brenda. She was good to us. And she was loving. So I didn't miss out on much."

Louanne had a feeling that being raised in luxury and affluence couldn't make up for what Rowan perceived as the loss of both his parents.

"Your dad was a very busy man who worked hard to provide for his family," she said, in an attempt to defuse some of his anger, his pain.

Rowan clicked his tongue. "Walter Parks worked

hard to commandeer an empire for himself to rule over. The man is a spider, keeping his employees and his family within his web of control."

"Do Emily and Cade feel the same way?"

"I have a younger sister, too. Jessica." Rowan blew out a ragged breath. "I'm not entirely sure how the others feel. As I grew up, it became obvious that when my father did come around, he favored my brother."

Louanne held her tongue, letting Rowan bare his soul. His pain. His resentment.

"For as long as I can remember, I was shoved aside to make room for Cade. And by the time I'd reached adolescence, I'd grown to hate my dad. So I rebelled, doing everything I could to make head-lines that would embarrass the man."

"What kind of things?" she asked.

"Nothing serious enough to be a felony, if that's what you mean."

That *was* what she meant. She'd already gotten in-volved with one man who had a criminal bent, even if Richard appeared to be a pillar of the academic community and hadn't ever stepped foot in a jail or prison. And she wasn't ready to involve herself with another one. Not that she and Rowan were involved, but they sure seemed to be leaning in that direction.

"I had my share of high school suspensions," Rowan said. "The last one came when I borrowed a buddy's motorcycle and raced around the football field. The janitor had already lined the lanes with lime for an upcoming track meet, and I drove over the top of them, screwing them up."

Why did she find his rebellion so intriguing? She blamed her curiosity on the renewal of her dreams, or being a budding novelist who studied the workings of character development and internal conflict. But, she suspected, deep inside, she very much wanted to know what made Rowan Parks tick for personal reasons. "Did you make it through high school?"

He nodded. "My grades were pretty decent, in spite of the trouble I got into."

"What about college?"

"My old man was determined I go to UCLA, but I kept forgetting to send in my application." Rowan tossed her a wry grin. "I procrastinated a lot, particularly when my dad told me to do something. But I did want an education."

"So you went to UCLA?"

"Yeah. My application arrived late, so in order to get me admitted, dear old dad had to pull strings and call in some favors—something he thrives on."

Louanne hadn't dealt with emotional issues with her parents, not like that. But she'd been champing at the bit to get out of Pebble Creek and spread her wings. "I'd think you would have liked moving away and going to college."

"I wasn't home much anyway. But it was good to get away from the high-society digs in San Francisco, where I was considered a black sheep. I think that my dad was glad to see me go, too. But I continued to infuriate him by getting into whatever trouble I could."

"What kind of trouble?"

"I was involved in a couple of pranks that some people might consider petty theft. And then there were a few panty raids."

"Did you graduate?"

"Nope. I wasn't looking for that kind of education. Besides, my dad quit paying my tuition, after one of my bigger scandals."

"Don't stop now." She slid him a tolerant smile, wanting to prod him on. "What kind of scandal?"

Rowan took a deep breath and blew it out. "Older women have always found me attractive."

Louanne didn't find that surprising. Rowan was drop-dead gorgeous, and she would have been sorely tempted to have an affair with him, if she would have known him back then. In fact, she was sorely tempted now.

"I'm not proud of this, but I was…" He paused for a moment, as though choosing his words. "Let's just say I became romantically involved with a politician's wife. And it resulted in a photograph of us in a compromising position. I'd be surprised if you didn't remember reading about the whole sordid affair. Some rather interesting versions of it made all the major supermarket tabloids. People in my dad's circle still whisper about it, especially since the politician lost his bid for reelection."

"I take it your dad was upset."

"He was furious. Especially since he'd been the man's top political supporter and had made a hefty contribution to the reelection campaign." Rowan glanced at Louanne to see how she had taken his admission.

She studied the hands she held clasped in her lap.

Had he shocked her? Disappointed her? He hoped not, but for some reason, it felt good to come clean, to admit all that stuff he'd bottled up for years.

But he didn't want to feel better if it meant losing Louanne's respect.

During that half-assed stint in college, pretty coeds had flocked around him. And even now, he had his choice of relationships. But he'd never spilled his guts in front of any of them. Not like this.

Louanne was different than the others, yet he still hated to reveal his vulnerability. The shame he felt when other people talked about their childhoods, their parents.

She glanced up from her musing. "Is that when you met Sam?"

Rowan nodded. "I already told you about how the guy gave me a purpose in life and encouraged me to set some goals and to dream. When Sam dragged his feet about starting a business with me, I bought a small place in Napa, where I built my own carpentry shop over the garage. And it wasn't long before I earned enough to tell my father what he could do with the damned trust fund he kept threatening to revoke."

"I'd think your dad would be proud of your carpentry skills." She offered him a smile, but it didn't warm the cold knot in Rowan's gut.

"I've become a master carpenter and have my own shop. I've got a business that's become lucrative. But that's always been my secret. Emily and Jessica know that I love working with wood, that I make toys for the kids at the homeless shelter and used to, before I left, help with carpentry on the family estate. But that's about it."

"Are you close to your sisters?" she asked.

"Yeah. But that's not a good enough reason for me to go back to California. The night I left my family, I got so angry with my old man, I couldn't see straight." Rowan pressed his eyes shut, wishing he could block out the painful scene and shove it back into his subconscious.

But it remained, just as clear as the night it had happened.

Walter Parks had called a family meeting and accused someone of talking about family business to outsiders. The accusation had been voiced to all of them. But the patriarch had been looking at Rowan. *I've hired a private detective. If I find any of you have talked about the family or the business, I'll see that you're cut off without a penny.*

It had been the last straw. *Afraid we'll let the world*

know our mother is in a lunatic asylum in a foreign land? Rowan asked. *Afraid someone will find out your diamond dealing isn't as up-and-up as you would have everyone believe?*

Walter surged to his feet. *Shut your mouth, boy, or I'll shut it for you. I wouldn't be surprised if you were stirring up trouble just for the hell of it.*

Rowan looked at Louanne, wondering how much more he should tell her. Should he reveal family secrets? Should he tell her of his suspicion regarding his father's business practices?

He chose to keep quiet about that—but *not* because of his father's threat. Walter Parks and the whole damn empire he'd created shamed him. "When I stormed out of my old man's house and took off on my bike, I wanted to escape my family indefinitely and find my own way in the world—a place where no one knew me. And that's how I ended up in Texas."

Louanne took his hand, and he caressed her roughened red skin with his thumb. He wished she wouldn't work so hard, that she could enjoy simple luxuries like a weekly manicure.

As he continued to stroke her warm flesh, he felt that familiar pull. The growing desire to take her in his arms and kiss her thoroughly, to make love until dawn. To make everything right in her world, even if he hadn't ever been able to make it right in his own.

He placed a kiss on the underside of her wrist,

where he could feel her steady heartbeat escalate. She was a good woman and deserved so much better than this ranch, so much better than him. "I'll leave, if you'd like me to."

Her brow furrowed. "Why would I want you to leave?"

He shrugged. "I don't know. Maybe because you've got a kid to raise and I've been a hellion my whole life. And a lost soul."

"Do lost souls seek each other out?" She gave his hand a squeeze, then pulled her grip from his. "Don't answer that. I'm not even sure why I asked."

Louanne excused herself and left Rowan sitting in the living room. He picked up a gaudy, tarnished-silver picture frame and looked at a photograph of an older couple he didn't know. He smiled back at them, then replaced the heavy frame where he found it.

He leaned back in the tweed sofa and contemplated his options, his future.

Could he rebuild his life in Pebble Creek? With Louanne and Noah?

The thought didn't scare him nearly as much as he expected it to.

The days passed, with Rowan going out and helping Pete on the ranch, doing lots of odds and ends, but mostly mending something. The place was falling apart before their very eyes.

In the evening, after dinner, Louanne would boot

up her laptop and write, while Rowan and Noah did dishes and played around until bedtime. The baby was getting steadier on his feet by the minute. And it seemed as though Noah was growing more and more attached to Rowan.

It warmed Rowan's rebel heart to see the kid light up like a casino on the Vegas strip each time he entered the room.

Rowan and Louanne had fallen easily into the roles of man and woman, mother and father. Even husband and wife—minus the sex, of course, but not the attraction.

They steered clear of touching each other, but a heated charge electrified the atmosphere whenever they moved within arm's length of each other. Hell, it sparked and flashed whenever their eyes met.

And quite frankly, Rowan was getting tired of avoiding the issue. He wanted Louanne something fierce, and if his instincts were any good—and they were—she wanted him, too.

This morning, after passing her in the hall on his way from the shower, after seeing her hair loose and free of the braid, after brushing against her denim-clad hip, catching a whiff of the peppermint tooth-paste she'd used, he damn near grabbed hold of her and kissed her senseless.

He hadn't, though—mostly because Noah had started fussing from his crib and Rowan didn't have the time to kiss her as thoroughly as he'd wanted.

But he didn't plan to fight the urge much longer.

While working out in the south pasture with Pete, the sun beating down on his back, and the fresh air taunting his senses, Rowan decided to do something about the passion brewing between him and Louanne.

"Do you and Aggie have plans for this evening?" he asked the older man.

Pete lifted the worn Stetson from his head, then swiped an arm across his sweaty brow. "Nothing out of the ordinary. What's on your mind?"

"I'd like you to keep Noah for a while." Rowan wasn't sure if the older man knew exactly what was on his mind, but to be on the safe side, he added, "I'd like to take Louanne into town for dinner."

"She won't go," Pete said. "But it's a nice thought, and I guess it won't hurt to ask her."

If Louanne said no, Rowan had another plan in the works. He'd make a romantic dinner for two—under the stars and away from the run-down ranch house that had become a prison of her own making.

It had been a long time since Rowan had seduced a woman. And even then, the idea hadn't been half as arousing as the thought of making love with Louanne.

"Aggie and I are taking off tomorrow on our road trip," Pete said, "so it'll be nice to spend some time with Noah this evening. In fact, he goes to sleep pretty early. Why don't we keep him overnight so you don't have to haul him back to Louanne's place? Aggie has a crib for him in our spare room."

"Sounds like a great idea to me." Rowan went back to work, eager for the sun to set.

He had plans for the evening.

And if all went well, he hoped his dinner plans would last until breakfast.

Chapter Eleven

After working all day in the sun, mending fences with Pete and building up an honest, feel-good sweat, Rowan entered the house through the service porch door and found Louanne in the kitchen. She'd just pulled a cast-iron skillet from the cupboard. A butcher-wrapped package sat on the counter.

She looked up when he walked in, her eyes lingering on him, just as his remained on her. A wisp of honey-brown hair had escaped the braid she always wore and rested along her cheek. She opened her mouth, as though she wanted to say something, but didn't speak.

And neither did he. He was content to bask in the sensual, pheromone-spiked aura that surrounded them, to study her simple, down-home beauty.

Her eyes lit up and her lips curled, setting off something warm and fluttery in his chest.

How could a woman dressed in faded jeans and worn cotton turn him inside out with a smile?

Rowan wouldn't say that Louanne was the most beautiful woman he'd ever seen, but she was by far the most attractive, the most intriguing. And she was the only one who'd reached deep inside of him, touching something soft and hidden.

He wanted to sweep her into his arms, give her a Baby-I'm-home kiss, then ask how her day was and tell her all about his. He wanted to place his hand possessively upon the curve of her hip, pull her close and let her know he planned to make love all night long.

Sheesh. Could he get any sappier than that?

He broke eye contact and scanned the kitchen, trying to put his thoughts in perspective. "Where's Noah?"

"Aggie took him for a walk. So I thought I'd fix dinner. I hope quesadillas and a taco salad sound all right with you."

"Actually," he began, "Pete said he and Aggie would baby-sit for us this evening. So I was wondering if you'd like to go into town and have dinner with me."

His question must have surprised her, because her lips parted and her eyes widened before she responded. "Thanks for asking. But I'm not up for dinner in a restaurant."

He could certainly see where Pete and Aggie had

gotten the idea that Louanne didn't like going into town. But Rowan didn't want to take no for an answer. "Then would you mind if I borrowed the truck and brought dinner to you?"

She paused, as though taken aback by his question, then glanced down at the empty skillet and the butcher-wrapped package. "Sure, if you want to. I can put the hamburger back in the fridge and fix it tomorrow night."

"Great. How about we have dinner somewhere away from the house? We'll stay on the Lazy B property, if that makes you feel better."

Her brow furrowed. "What do you have in mind?"

"A nighttime picnic."

She cocked her head to the side and, although the hint of a grin surfaced, she eyed him suspiciously. "In the dark?"

He figured a little starlight and candles ought to offer enough visibility. And if not? "We can always use the headlamps of the pickup, if necessary."

Her face scrunched in an adorable little girl expression—like the one his younger sister Jessica had worn whenever Rowan teased her while they were growing up. "Are you serious about this?"

He nodded, unable to keep his lips from quirking in a silly, uncontrollable grin or his hormones from kicking into overdrive. "I figured we could both use a change of scenery." *Not to mention a night alone.*

She seemed to ponder his words, but not for very

long. "All right. I have to admit, I don't have much opportunity for adventure anymore."

Well, he hoped she was up for a *romantic* adventure, because that's what he had in mind.

"There's one more thing," he said. "Let's get dressed up for the evening."

She crossed her arms, the yellow-and-green material of her blouse stretching snug, revealing the swell of her breasts, something he missed seeing when she wore loose-fitting work shirts. Would she choose the green slinky dress he'd bought her? Would she let her hair down?

It didn't matter, he supposed. As long as she agreed to the out-of-the-ordinary date, she could wear what she had on now.

"You want me to get all dressed up for a picnic?" she asked.

"Nighttime picnics are pretty formal." He tossed a smile her way. "So, if you'll excuse me, I'm going to take a shower first. Then I'll head into town."

She placed her hands on her denim-clad hips and studied him carefully. Those golden-brown eyes glimmered with what looked like excitement.

Good. He was excited, too.

She opened a cupboard by the refrigerator, pulled a leather-fobbed key ring from a hook on the inside of the door and handed it to him. "Here are the keys to the truck, just in case I'm not out of the bath when you're ready to leave."

It took all Rowan had not to sweep her into his arms and give her a hot, star-spinning, knee-weakening kiss as a prelude to what he had planned. But he would wait until the time was right. If they made love tonight, and he hoped they would, the suggestion would come from her.

He lifted the keys to the truck. "Thanks, Louanne. You won't be disappointed."

And he wasn't just talking about tonight's menu or the romantic setting.

Louanne sat on the quilted blanket Rowan had placed on a grassy knoll not far from the creek. The sun had long since dropped out of sight. And they'd eaten the last morsel of the roast beef dinner from the Bluebonnet Café, but she was in no hurry to go home.

Rowan Parks was amazing. Not just because of his devilish good looks and witty conversation, but because he'd gone out of his way to make the evening more than special.

His efforts might be a bit rustic, but they were very romantic. He'd taken an old wooden crate out of the truck and turned it over to use as a table. He'd gathered the paper plates they'd used and put them in a trash bag, but the makeshift dining table still held a half-empty bottle of merlot, three paper cups—one sporting a single red rose—and a candle that cast an enchanting aura on the evening.

The flickering candlelight merely added to the

ambiance already cast by the magical glimmer of a star-studded sky.

Crickets chirped, and a barn owl hooted. Down by the creek, bullfrogs croaked in lure of a mate, harmonizing in what surely was God's idea of a lover's concerto.

Lovers?

She and Rowan weren't lovers.

But it felt as though they were. And the night Rowan had created for her, or rather for them, was more romantic than Louanne had ever imagined, setting a warm glow in her heart and arousing more than a little sexual interest.

"Would you like to dance?" Rowan asked.

She lifted a brow and slid him an easy smile. "To the sounds of Mother Nature?"

He rose from the quilt, then pulled the keys from his pocket as he strode for the truck. He opened the door, reached for the ignition and the radio, fiddling with the dial until he found a station out of Austin that played soft rock. A sultry love song soon filled the night air, and Rowan returned to where she sat and extended a hand.

This was crazy. Silly. But too darn tempting to resist. Louanne took his hand and got to her feet. His arms slipped around her, and she leaned into his embrace, laid her head against his cheek, inhaled his musky scent. She closed her eyes and lost herself in the moment.

They swayed like that for the longest time, letting the words and melody take them to a special place—a place she'd never been. A place she didn't want to leave.

"Rowan?"

His steps slowed, and he loosened his hold long enough to look her in the eye, to listen to what she had to say.

He'd been so gentlemanly, so considerate, so darn attractive and appealing, that the heat brewing in his eyes came as a welcome surprise and set off a surge of desire and need.

For reasons she wouldn't ponder now, she pulled his mouth to hers.

Rowan had wondered whether Louanne would ever make the first move, but he'd been determined to let her call the shots. After all, she had the most to lose if things didn't work out between them. But this was more than a date, more than a seduction. And he hoped she wanted to make love as badly as he did.

Without any conscious effort on his part, their kiss deepened, breaths mingled and hands caressed. Blood pumped in all the right places, causing more than a growing arousal. It stirred a desperate need that ought to scare the heck out of him. But it didn't.

The only thing he feared was having her pull away, having her put a stop to their foreplay, because he didn't want to let her go, didn't want things to remain platonic between them.

But he refused to think about anything other than this kiss, this evening and pleasuring the lady in his arms.

Their tongues danced in a slow, primal mating ritual, taking and giving, in a rhythm set by beating hearts and surging hormones.

He couldn't imagine anything he wanted more than to make love with Louanne, out here under the watchful eye of the moon and stars. Alone with nature and free of constraints.

But he wanted their lovemaking to be her idea.

And heaven help him if she didn't want him as badly as he wanted her.

Louanne threaded her fingers through Rowan's hair, drawing closer to him, deepening the kiss and stoking the fire that blazed between them. She leaned into his arousal, felt the hard evidence of his need for her, while increasing her own need for him.

She hadn't meant to kiss Rowan again, to let things take a sexual turn. But in spite of her reservations and her fears, she wanted to take all he had to offer and give everything she had to share.

Whether it was the romantic spell of a Texas summer night or the dark-haired rebel whose kiss drove her wild, she wasn't sure. All she knew was that she wanted him. Wanted this.

Louanne yearned to feel his skin against hers, to explore his body with her hands and her mouth, while he explored hers. And she yearned to feel him slip deep inside of her.

She broke the kiss and caught his gaze. "Do you want this as badly as I do?"

He nodded. "Probably more so."

"Here?" she asked, nodding toward the blanket that awaited them.

He smiled, sending a flush of warm shivers through her veins, then took her hand and led her back to the quilt.

He didn't kiss her again, didn't lay her down. He merely watched her, appreciation burning in his eyes. The stars seemed brighter than they had only moments ago, the night more alive. Her senses were more alert, her desire more intense.

She kicked off her shoes and dropped to her knees on the blanket. He joined her, eyes locked, hearts undoubtedly beating in unison.

If it were possible, now that she'd set things in motion, she wanted him all the more.

He took her hand and kissed it as if she were a princess and not a ranch hand with chapped hands. But she couldn't fall into the Lord and Lady roles as easily as that. She made a fist, trying to hide the red, roughened skin, and pulled her hand free.

"What's the matter?" he asked.

"I don't know." She glanced at the blanket, then back at him. "Self-conscious, I guess."

"Why?"

"My hands used to be soft. And my nails were longer, filed evenly. And now?" She shook her head.

He took her hand again and slowly unfurled the fingers, kissing each one. "You're beautiful to me. Inside and out."

The sincerity of his gaze validated his words, touching something deep in her heart. She reached for him, and they came together in a lover's quest, searching, seeking. Prolonging each touch, each taste.

He reached for the hem of her cotton sundress, and she moved with him to help lift it over her head, leaving her wearing only a pair of white panties and a bra. He brushed his mouth against hers, then kissed her throat, leaving hot, breathy kisses along her skin.

Her nipples hardened, and she unhooked her bra, letting it drop to the ground.

"Ah, honey." His voice was low and husky, laden with desire and filled with appreciation. He cupped her breasts, his thumbs taunting her responsive nipples and nearly sending her over the edge.

"I'm not sure how long I can wait," she told him. "I want you inside me."

He must have heard her, but he lowered his head, kissing her breasts, laving one nipple and then the other until she whimpered with need.

When he looked up and caught her eye, desire flashed between them.

She fumbled with the buttons of his shirt, until he began to help, then she reached for the top metal button of his pants. Moments later, they were both naked, lying on the quilt, caught up in a fire that raged out of control.

Rowan rolled to the side, reached into the pocket of his discarded jeans and withdrew a foil packet. He put on a condom, then hovered over her, eyes glazed with passion.

Louanne didn't think she could wait a moment longer before feeling him inside her. "I'm aching for you."

As he entered her, she rose to meet each thrust until the stars spun out of control. She cried out with her climax, a primal response she'd never had before.

Her cry merely drove him on, sending him over the same peak. He shuddered with the strength of his own release, and she pulled him close, content to bask in the afterglow of an incredibly sweet joining.

As they lay on the blanket, wrapped in each others' arms, harmonious waves of pleasure soothed them both.

Sated for the time being and feeling more fulfilled than ever before, Louanne lay still, afraid to blink, to speak, to break the magic of what they'd shared.

Rowan rolled slowly to the side, taking her with him. When their eyes met, something passed between them. Something that filled her heart and nearly took her breath away.

She didn't mention it though. Didn't dare throw

the heady thought of love into the newness of a mind-swirling mix of emotions. She placed her hand upon his cheek, felt the light bristle of his beard.

He smiled, sending her heart topsy-turvy again. But rather than let go and roll with the feeling, she struggled with the intimacy, with trusting someone enough to let him into a heart that had once been betrayed.

Or was it too late?

Had she already fallen head over heels for a hell-bent rebel who'd just taken her to heaven and back?

When Rowan and Louanne returned to the house, neither of them mentioned sleeping in the same bed, but that's what Rowan had in mind. He wanted to hold Louanne all night long, loving her again and again.

They hadn't talked about tomorrow. About what the future held for either of them when morning dawned. And Rowan wasn't sure he wanted to. Not yet. Not while his body was still resonating from the best sex he'd ever had.

But it was just as well. He was still tiptoeing around his feelings, trying to figure out what kind of hold Louanne had on him.

She excused herself and went into the bathroom, while he took a seat in the living room. He supposed they would talk about sleeping arrangements when she returned.

The telephone rang, and he glanced at his watch. It was nearly eleven.

"Can you please answer that for me?" Louanne called out. "It might be Aggie."

"Sure." He snatched the receiver. "Hello."

No answer.

"Hello?"

Still no answer. A heavy click sounded on the other end, disconnecting the line. A wrong number, he supposed.

Moments later, the phone rang again.

This time, Rowan answered in a clipped voice. "Hello."

Still no response. Was the caller's telephone on the blink? Or was this a prank call?

Breathing sounded on the other end. Damn. He hated when that happened. *Speak up or hang up.*

Fed up and not willing to mess around with a jerk, Rowan plopped the receiver down on the cradle. In his haste, he bumped the heavy, ornate picture frame of that smiling older couple—Louanne's parents, he assumed—and nearly knocked it to the floor.

Five minutes later, the telephone rang again. He had half a notion to ignore the damn thing, but it wasn't his house, his phone. Or his decision. So, in no mood for games, he grabbed the receiver again. "Who the hell is this?"

"Rowan?" his older sister's voice asked.

"Emily?"

"Yes, it's me. What's going on?"

"Sorry, Em. We've had a couple of prank calls. I thought yours might be another one."

"How are you doing?" Her voice sounded strained. Tentative. Awkward.

"I'm okay."

"Louanne said you had an accident."

"My bike was banged up." He didn't tell her that he'd been banged up, too. Emily always did worry about him. Sometimes too much. "I'm doing all right."

"Good. I…uh…called to check on you."

"I appreciate your concern." And he did. His problem was with his father, not his brother and sisters. But returning to the family fold wasn't an option.

"Dad shouldn't have made that accusation. And I understand why you were angry."

He didn't respond. Emily knew as well as he did that the final accusation had merely been the last straw.

"I wish there was something I could do to make things right."

"You can't, Emily. No one can." No one but Walter Parks, and it was too late for that.

"I also called to tell you some news."

"What kind of news?"

"Conrad and Tyler Carlton claim that our father had an affair with their mother."

So what? It didn't surprise Rowan to hear something like that. He'd never thought of his father as an honorable man. And when Walter Parks wanted something, he went after it. If the wife of a business associate had caught Walter's eye, Rowan suspected the jewelry baron wouldn't have let something like a marriage vow stand in his way. "Are the Carltons asking for money?"

"They're demanding DNA testing."

From what Rowan remembered, Marla Carlton had given birth to the twins months after her husband's accidental drowning twenty-five years ago. Had Walter fathered her babies?

Rowan didn't doubt it. Was the extramarital affair the secret Walter had accused Rowan of revealing? Probably so, although who knew what kind of skeletons Walter had in his closet.

A wry grin tugged at his lips. He actually relished the problems a paternity suit and the resulting publicity would cause his father. "If Conrad and Tyler try to claim a portion of the Parks Empire, good ol' dad isn't going to be too happy."

"He's upset," Emily said. "But there's not much he can do about it. He received a subpoena for a blood test and complied. If the results prove he's their father, it will be common knowledge soon."

"Well, for their sake," Rowan said, "I hope the test comes back negative. I wouldn't wish a father like Walter Parks on anyone."

The garbage from the past clogged the telephone line. But they didn't discuss the wealth-and-power-driven patriarch any further than that.

What was there to say? Emily knew how Rowan felt about the man. And there wasn't much she could do to hold the family together now.

If Rowan actually gave a rat's ass about his standing in the family, he might wonder what a paternity revelation like that would do. But he didn't give a damn anymore. He was beyond caring about anything that affected those caught up in the mighty Parks dynasty.

Of course, that didn't mean he wasn't glad his sister had called. But he wanted nothing more to do with his family. He planned to rebuild his life, to succeed on his own. And Pebble Creek seemed like a good place to start over.

"How long will you be in Texas?" Emily asked.

Rowan supposed that was her way of skirting the real questions she had. Are you coming back home? Have you gotten over the blowup this time? Or did the old man finally drive you away for good?

"I'm going to return to San Francisco," he answered, "but only long enough to pack up and put my house on the market."

His sister didn't respond. And he knew why. The ongoing rift had become too deep, and she knew how stubborn and adamant Rowan could be when prodded. And she knew better than to push him on the issue.

"Well, I'll let you go," Emily said. "Please give me a call now and then, just to let me know how you're doing."

"I will." Rowan didn't mean to shut out his siblings entirely, but he wasn't going to live within Walter's web of control any longer.

"I'll keep you posted," Emily said. "You know. About how things are going around here. And about the paternity issue."

The line grew silent and heavy. Rowan wanted to tell her not to bother. To just leave him the hell out of any family concerns or issues—good or bad. But Emily didn't deserve his anger. Nor did she deserve to listen to him vent about things that would never change. "Thanks for the call, Em."

He meant what he said, but that didn't allay the pent-up anger. The urge to slam his fist into a wall.

Grief was a process, the TV shrink had said. It passed with time. Did anger and resentment pass as well?

The line had disconnected long before Rowan hung up the telephone.

Louanne cleared her throat, and he spotted her in the doorway. A white cotton nightgown reflected her innocence and made him want to reach for her, to bury himself in her sweet goodness and put the ugly past behind him.

"Who was on the telephone?" she asked.

"My sister, Emily."

"Is something wrong?"

Wrong? Other than the fact Rowan's life had never felt right, even as a kid. Or the fact that he might have two illegitimate half brothers who didn't have any idea what they might be setting themselves up for?

No. There was nothing wrong—other than the fact Rowan felt ready to explode, to burst out in foul language or pain-induced tears.

But that wasn't Louanne's fault, so he tried to put it all behind him. "Emily asked how long I planned to stay here. But I think she wanted to know whether I planned to go back home."

"What did you tell her?" Louanne lifted a hand to the front of her gown, her fingers fiddling with a button and a satin ribbon.

Did she want him to stay? Here on the ranch with her? Or at least nearby in Pebble Creek?

Or did the thought of him setting down roots worry her?

They hadn't taken time to discuss the future yet. And Louanne certainly didn't know enough about his past to understand why he would never step foot on the Parks estate again.

So he merely answered her question as simply and truthfully as he could. "I have no intention of ever going home. Not to the family estate."

Louanne's heart ached for Rowan and his father, as well as their entire family. As badly as she wanted him to stay and make a life with her on the ranch, to dream and pretend everything was right in her world—in their world—she couldn't.

There was no way she could stand by as Rowan severed all ties with his father.

There were so many things she wished she would have told her parents, so many things she could have done for them and *with* them, if she still had a chance to do so.

"Sometimes things are said in the heat of the moment," she told him, "things that are cruel and hurtful. Maybe you should give your father a call and try to talk to him and set things right."

"I *did* set things right when I left. I cut all the skimpy ties we might have had. And I don't plan to ever speak to that bastard again." Rowan's eyes narrowed and his lips tensed.

Louanne hated to prod him, so she let him ponder her words while she locked all the doors in the house, something her parents never had to do at night, but something that had become her habit since moving home.

When she returned to the living room, she found Rowan staring out the window and into the night.

He might want her to believe the serious rift with his father was none of her business. But she wasn't so sure.

And she could no longer take a passive stance.

She made her way across the floor and slipped her arms around his waist, rested her cheek against his back and savored his musky scent. "I don't mean to interfere."

He didn't turn around, didn't speak.

"But I'm afraid you'll be sorry some day, if you don't try and rectify things now."

Rowan took a deep breath and turned around. His eyes caught hers, but they weren't filled with vulnerability. They sparked in anger. "I appreciate you trying to help, to understand. But you can't. That man is dead to me, as far as I'm concerned."

"I'm sorry you feel that way. I wish you'd reconsider. He's the only father you have."

The luck of a bad draw, if you asked Rowan. He crossed his arms, unwilling to go into his reasons any further. Why wouldn't she just let it drop?

"Back off, Louanne. This is none of your business." His words sounded harsh, even to him. But so were his memories of the painful relationship he'd had with his father.

She stiffened and stood taller.

He ought to backpedal, say something to appease her, but angry and hurt from years of emotional neglect and abuse, he reverted to his natural way of dealing with conflict—clamming up and walking away.

"If you'll excuse me," he said, trying to be more considerate than he would have been to anyone else who'd dared to stir up his pain. "I'm going to bed."

Then he turned and walked away, his footsteps clicking on the hardwood flooring in the hall.

When he got to his room, or rather the guest room

that had once belonged to Louanne's sister, he closed the door.

But this time the barrier didn't work.

Instead of steeling himself against the pain, he felt it all the more.

Chapter Twelve

Rowan had slept like hell.

In the past, once he'd shut someone or something out, he hadn't stewed about the decision. And he'd damn sure never lost any sleep over it.

Heck, turning his back and walking away was what he did best; he closed doors and burned bridges—a defensive response that had always worked.

But not last night.

Shutting out Louanne hadn't helped at all. And in fact, it had made him feel worse, leaving his emotions ragged and frayed.

But she'd asked too much of him. She wanted him to salvage a bridge he planned to burn. And by refusing, Rowan was burning the bridge he and Louanne were building to connect their own lives. And that wasn't something he wanted to destroy. Not before he had a chance to see where it led.

So what were his options?

He could give in and beg his father for forgiveness, just as Louanne had prodded him to do, but Rowan didn't have anything to apologize for. And even if he did, Walter Parks thrived on having the upper hand. For that reason, Rowan would rather jump a barbed wire fence naked than bow down before his old man.

Maybe he should level with Louanne, open up and spill his guts, tell her how damn much it had hurt to grow up under Walter Parks's roof and completely out of the man's favor.

And while he was at it, he could bare his heart and soul to her.

Oh, yeah? And tell her what? That he felt something for her? That he might even love her? That he was sorry for turning his back on her and responding in a manner that was natural for him?

Rowan kicked off the covers and climbed out of bed. What he needed was a shower. Maybe the pounding spray of water would free his mind and trigger a few options he hadn't thought of. He grabbed a clean pair of jeans from the closet and headed for the bathroom.

But a shower hadn't helped, either.

As he stood before the fogged mirror with a damp towel around his waist and a razor in his hand, he hadn't come up with anything—other than apologizing to Louanne.

That would certainly be a first. Rowan wasn't one to offer explanations or say "I'm sorry." And he wasn't sure where an admission like that would leave him.

Or them.

After he dressed, he went in search of the woman who'd turned his life on end—even before their disagreement. He found her in the kitchen, standing over a pot of oatmeal on the stove. She turned when he entered, dark circles under her eyes bearing testimony to the fretful night she'd spent.

A sense of guilt hovered over him. He didn't like being the cause of her restless sleep. Or the reason for her sadness. "I'm sorry, Louanne."

There was so much more left to say, to explain. And he wondered if she knew how difficult this sort of thing was for him.

Maybe so, because she turned down the flame, placed the wooden spoon she held on the countertop and joined him in the doorway—meeting him halfway, he supposed. Another first, as far as he was concerned.

Without a conscious thought, his arms opened for her, and she leaned into his embrace. He pulled her close, trying to find comfort and balance, as he inhaled the citrus scent of her shampoo and savored her gentle touch. "I don't want this thing with my family to come between us."

She brushed a kiss against his cheek. "I'm sorry, for dredging up those old hurts."

He took her hand and led her into the living room, then sat beside her on the sofa. "I've never been one to talk about stuff that bothers me. Not to anyone."

"I wish you'd share those feelings with me."

Yeah. He did, too. But how did he start? At the beginning? Did he dare voice the crux of his pain?

He took a breath, then slowly blew it out. "My father never loved me. Not ever."

Never? As a parent, Louanne found that hard to believe. Perhaps Rowan and his father had been estranged for so long, that Rowan couldn't remember the love they'd once shared. Wanting to help without pushing him, like she'd done last night, she kept quiet and let him continue.

Rowan cleared his throat, as though needing to dislodge the words. "I don't know. Maybe I remind my father of my mother. Or maybe my old man never wanted children."

It was possible, she supposed. But it was just as likely that things had become so strained between father and son during Rowan's adolescent years that they'd both forgotten the good times. Surely, there'd been some happy memories.

Rowan fingered the scar over his left brow, as though it still bothered him. "Kids need more than an estate to live in. More than fancy toys and gadgets to keep a rich child entertained."

True. But life in a run-down ranch house left a bit to be desired, too. Again, she held her tongue.

"I like to think that my mother loved me. But I can't actually remember her. And Brenda, our nanny, loved me. But it wasn't enough. My father was too busy building an empire to be bothered with his kids. And on those rare occasions when he came home before bedtime, he used to shove me aside—something he never seemed to do with Cade."

"I'm sure your teenage rebellion didn't help the relationship any."

"Probably not. But at the time, I dealt with it the only way I knew how." Rowan turned toward her. His knee brushed hers, connecting them, but not nearly enough. "Whenever there was a problem at home, my father always blamed me. And I'm still his scapegoat. The night I left the estate in anger, he'd accused me of revealing family secrets, of being a traitor."

Louanne reached out and took his hand. "I think you need to settle things with your father, even if that means confronting him and finding some closure. Otherwise, you'll never truly be happy."

Was she right? Did he need to make some kind of peace with the past so he could face the future without the burden of an anger and resentment he couldn't shake?

Sam had once suggested Rowan sit down with his

dad and have a man-to-man conversation, telling his father that they should agree to disagree, that they could end their cold war by trying to coexist without making each other's life miserable.

Rowan hadn't given that piece of advice any consideration. But the two people he cared about the most in this world had said nearly the same thing.

"I'm not sure whether I can make amends with my father. And I don't know if I really want to. But you're right. I need to have some closure." Rowan stood and shoved his hands in his pockets, afraid to assume his and Louanne's budding relationship would last while he faced his dad and tried to put the past behind him.

He was even more afraid to ask Louanne whether they had a chance of making some kind of life together. But this seemed to be a good time to face his fears and apprehensions.

"I'm not making any promises," he said, "but my resentment toward my father has affected my relationship with my brother and sisters. I left that night, not planning to have anything to do with any of them again."

"The resentment you hold toward your father will probably affect every relationship you ever have."

He knew what she meant. His relationship with Louanne didn't stand a chance if he didn't put his past to rest. "In that case, I'm going to catch a flight to San Francisco today. But when I come back, I want to talk about the future, not the past."

"Your future?" she asked.

"Our future. If you and Noah would like to build one with me."

A grin burst forth, lighting her eyes. "We'll have to talk about that, after you've taken care of old business." Then she stood and offered him a hug.

It didn't seem like enough fortification for the trip ahead. But he wouldn't ask her for more. Not yet. But the sooner he left, the sooner he'd get back.

He gave her a long, lingering kiss, one filled with memories of their last joining and hope for the future. A kiss that promised he'd be back.

She took a pad and pen from the drawer in the lamp stand, then wrote down her telephone number.

"I'll give you a call," he said. "Later."

"Thanks. I'll be here. Waiting." She slid him a doe-eyed smile that made him wonder if he ought to postpone his trip until after Pete and Aggie returned. But Louanne had made her point.

He nodded, then left the house and headed for the barn, where he found his Harley. As he pushed the bike into the yard, he spotted Pete walking toward the porch with Noah in his arms. The baby boy squealed when he saw Rowan, something that never failed to touch Rowan's rebel heart.

"Where are you off to?" the old man asked.

"I need to go back to California for a while."

"How long are you going to be gone?"

"Just a couple of days." Rowan hoped it wouldn't

be longer than that. "Or do you think I should stay until you get back?"

"Jim Collier, the man who owns the ranch to the east of us, said he'd watch over things. I did the same for him last year." Pete smiled, then nodded toward the house, toward Louanne. "You two have a nice evening?"

"Yeah." At least Rowan had thought so. Their lovemaking had been great. And promising—until they'd argued. Until she urged him to confront his father, and Rowan shut her out. But their reconciliation had set his life back on track. And he couldn't wait to get this trip to San Francisco behind him.

"Good. We were glad to have Noah last night. Aggie and I are leaving around noon." Pete chuckled and looked at the baby in his arms. "But I'm not sure Aggie will be able to stand being away from Noah very long."

Rowan could understand that. He was going to miss the little guy, too. Not to mention his pretty mom.

"You're coming back, aren't you?" Pete asked.

"Yeah. I have some things to clear up and work out. But I'll be back. And I plan to stick around for a while." Rowan slapped a hand on the older man's shoulder. "You and Aggie have a great time on that road trip. Be safe and take care."

Pete grinned and shifted Noah in his arms. "We plan to. You take care, too, son."

Son. It felt kind of nice coming from Pete. It

would have been even nicer had his old man ever referred to him as anything other than *boy*.

"Thanks. I'll do that." Rowan climbed on the bike. And after one last glance at the house, he revved the engine and sped off.

It was time to confront his past, he supposed.

Whether he wanted to or not.

Rowan hadn't been gone a full day, and already Louanne missed him something fierce. And to make matters worse, she'd had a teary-eyed farewell when Pete and Aggie had climbed into their motor home and driven away.

As the day wore on and nighttime settled on the ranch, Louanne's loneliness deepened.

Had Rowan arrived in San Francisco safely? Was everything all right? Would things between him and his dad grow worse? Had she been wrong to encourage him to try to make peace?

Several times throughout the evening, she'd reached for the notepad that held contact information for Emily and Brenda. But she fought the urge to call. Besides, if Rowan wanted to talk to her, he had her number. But that didn't make waiting any easier.

Their future together seemed to hinge on what was happening in San Francisco, but Louanne didn't want to interfere any more than she had already.

In spite of herself, she'd grown to love the dark-haired rebel. More than she'd imagined possible.

And there was still so much they had to talk about, so much to decide. Hope and renewed dreams kept her awake.

She rolled over, taking the sheet and lightweight blanket with her, as she tried to find a comfortable spot. Her bed seemed bigger and emptier than she remembered. Lonelier.

The telephone on the nightstand rang, and her heart leaped. It must be Rowan. She grabbed the receiver quickly, so Noah wouldn't wake. A catch in her voice betrayed her hope. "Hello?"

Heavy breathing sounded over the line.

Was Rowan finding it difficult to talk? To tell her what had happened? Was he struggling with his feelings? Or had he been hurt in an accident of some kind?

"Rowan? Is that you?"

No response. Just the same eerie, breath-filled silence.

A random, obscene phone call?

Uneasy, she hung up. Surely, the call had been just a prank. A typical case of some sicko getting a thrill from calling a stranger late at night and stirring up fear.

But she couldn't discount the other possibility.

Had Richard found her? Was this his way of harassing her?

No, she told herself. She'd been careful. She'd covered her tracks.

Still, apprehension settled over her.

She needed to talk to someone, to hear a

comforting voice on the line. Her first instinct was to call Rowan. But she didn't want to bother him. Besides, her imagination was probably doing a number on her. And her fear would probably prove to be unfounded.

Another option came to mind.

Louanne had confided in her sister earlier—sort of. She'd told Lula that a guy she'd been dating at college had become too attached, and that she'd gone home without giving him any idea of how to reach her.

"Just in case he tries to find me through you," Louanne had said, "I don't want you giving any information out about me or the ranch."

"Good grief, Lou. I've held on to a glamorous childhood for so long, I doubt that I could even find my way back home." Her sister had laughed in that bubbly way that made Louanne believe Lula had everything figured out and under control. "Why don't you and Noah come live with me in California?"

Louanne had declined because the limelight was something she'd wanted to avoid. Living in Beverly Hills, within the range of a bursting flashbulb, wasn't a good idea. Not when she needed to keep her whereabouts and Noah's existence a secret.

She fumbled through the nightstand drawer in search of her sister's number at the hotel in which she was staying. What chance did she have of finding Lula in her room?

There was only one way to find out.

When a man answered, Louanne introduced herself, and he passed the phone to her sister.

"Hey, Lou. How's my nephew?"

"He's walking now. And saying a few words." Louanne twirled the telephone cord around her finger. "You know, I've been thinking about your invitation to come and visit."

"Great."

"And if it's all right," Louanne added, "I might bring a friend."

"A friend?"

A smile tugged at Louanne's lips. "Just a man I've met."

Lula, who'd been paired with some of Hollywood's biggest male stars, laughed. "Well, I'm looking forward to meeting him. Tell me about him."

Louanne gave her sister a brief description, lingering more on the way Rowan made her feel than his appearance. "His name is Rowan Parks, and he's from San Francisco."

"San Francisco?" Lula asked. "He isn't part of the Parks jewelry empire, is he?"

"His family is in the jewelry business. He's a carpenter."

"You never have been attracted to glitz and glamour, not like me. But good job, honey." Lula let out a long, slow whistle. "Parks is the west coast equivalent of Tiffany's and makes other jewelry stores look like the five-and-dime."

"That wasn't what turned my head," Louanne said, her voice firm.

"No one knows that better than me. You've always been the romantic one." Lula laughed again. "Listen, sis, I have to go. We'll have to finish the conversation soon."

"I'll keep you posted on that visit."

"Good. I can't wait to see you again. Or to hug and kiss my nephew. And I'd like to check out that new man in your life."

After saying goodbye and ending the call, Louanne didn't feel much better. But to ensure a good night's sleep, she turned down the ringer on the telephone.

Rowan paused before the Poseidon fountain in the front courtyard of the opulent two-story mansion in which he'd grown up, remembering the day he'd put a bottle of dishwashing detergent in the water. The bubbles had swelled to a mountainous froth, running over the sides and into the drive. It had been a pretty cool sight, until his father roared his disapproval. Rowan had gotten a backhand that day, as well as a punishment. But he could still recall a ten-year-old boy's pride at getting to the old man.

But his days of pranks and scandals were over.

He walked toward the front steps, the soles of his leather boots clicking upon the flagstone. But just as he reached the outdoor staircase that led to the house, the door swung open.

His father and a young man Rowan didn't recognize stood in the doorway, bodies tense, eyes glaring, expressions hard.

The black-haired man who appeared to be in his twenties didn't seem to be the least bit intimidated by the formidable Walter Parks. And Rowan couldn't help admiring him for it.

"This isn't the end of my search," the younger man said.

Walter bristled, but didn't speak. He just stared at the man, as Rowan did.

The guy stood about six feet tall and had a muscular build and a cocky, don't-mess-with-me stance that Rowan liked.

As the man turned to go, his gaze met Rowan's. He didn't smile, but extended a hand in greeting. "I'm Tyler Carlton."

Rowan didn't have any beefs with the man who claimed to be his half brother, so he introduced himself and shook hands. He hadn't been trying to rebel or be disloyal. He was just being polite. But Walter didn't appear pleased with the courteous gesture.

When Tyler proceeded down the steps and to a car parked in the drive, Rowan continued his approach to the house. Walter must have been caught off guard by the younger man's visit, because he stepped aside and let Rowan enter without the usual click of the tongue or snap of a criticism.

"I'd like to talk to you," Rowan said. "If you don't mind."

"Join the club," Walter muttered. "Let's go into the library. I'm going to fix a stiff drink. Maybe two."

Rowan tried not to analyze what may or may not have happened before his arrival. His dog wasn't in that fight.

"You want something to drink?" his father asked, as they entered the massive room with a built-in bar.

"I'll have a beer." Rowan took a seat on the plush, leather sofa and watched as his father first poured a glass of Scotch, straight up, and reached for a beer in the refrigerator behind the bar.

"I thought the doctor told you to drink wine, instead of hard liquor."

"This is a special occasion," he said, a scowl belying his words. "And a good stiff drink seems more apropos than passing out cigars, don't you think?"

Had the test results come back? Is that what Tyler came by to talk to him about? Rowan would have had a snappy comment in the past, but he kept it to himself.

Walter handed Rowan his drink, then sank into a wingback chair. "What's on your mind?"

Rowan pondered his thoughts, as well as the best way to broach them. He wasn't looking for love any longer, just an end to the problems they'd had in the past. "Our relationship hasn't been good for years. And I thought we ought to clear up a few things."

Walter took a slow sip from his glass. "What kind of 'things?'"

"First of all, in case you haven't noticed, I keep to myself. And I'm secretive by nature. I don't open up easily. And I don't divulge anything that pertains to me personally or to this family. If someone has been telling tales out of school, it wasn't me."

Walter lifted his glass, watched the lamplight glimmer through the caramel-colored liquor, then looked at Rowan. "You've done your best to stir things up and create one problem after another for me. I'm sure you understand why I would suspect you first."

"That brings me to the second point. I'm not sure when our problems began. And I'm not about to re-hash them. But I'd like to put the past anger and resentment behind us."

"You've behaved like a hellion all through your teenage years and well into college."

"And you were never a father to me," Rowan countered, before taking a thirst-quenching swig from the longneck bottle. "So if we want to start throwing the rocks we've stored up over the years, we've both got an endless supply."

"That's for damn sure." Walter set his glass on a teakwood coaster that sat on the lamp table at his side, then, as if having second thoughts, picked it back up again and took a drink. "You know, I didn't set out to fail you. Or the others."

It was the first admission or hint of wrongdoing Rowan had ever remembered his father uttering. And quite frankly, it took him aback.

"Like everyone on this earth," Walter said. "I made mistakes."

"What kind of mistakes?"

"Just things I wish I'd done differently."

It was, Rowan realized, the first time he and his father had a conversation that wasn't loaded with hostility and accusations. They would probably never be close, but maybe Louanne had been right. Maybe he and his father could at least be cordial to one another.

"By the way," Walter said. "You have two brothers to acknowledge, Tyler and Conrad Carlton. According to the paternity test the court ordered, I fathered them."

Fathered? That was a stretch. Walter had merely been a sperm donor. But true to his decision to offer an olive branch, Rowan kept the thought to himself. If he felt any compassion over the test results, it was for the two men who had to claim Walter as a father.

Since Jeremy Carlton, their mother's husband, had died before the twins' birth, they'd grown up without a father's love, just as Rowan had.

Just as Noah would.

Unless, of course, Rowan stepped up to the plate and adopted him. The thought put the first bit of warmth in Rowan's heart since he'd left Pebble Creek. And he actually liked the idea. Would Louanne want Rowan to be a father to her son?

Unlike the women he'd dated in the past, Louanne was different. And so was Rowan—when he was with her. He'd softened, opened up. And being with Noah had touched something in Rowan, too. He actually enjoyed the family-like feelings that had settled around him since staying at the ranch.

In the past, he would have run from something like that. But not this time. He didn't even want to *walk* away from Louanne and Noah.

The family he'd always wanted was in Pebble Creek.

Rowan finished his beer, then looked at his father. At sixty years of age, Walter's dark hair was more salt than pepper. And the brown eyes that could grow so cold and ruthless seemed haunted and troubled now. In a way, it made Rowan feel a bit sorry for his father—but just a tad. "Like I said, we'll probably never be close. But I want you to know that my days of stirring up trouble to set your life on end are over."

Walter nodded. "I'm glad to hear it."

Rowan had never shared much of anything with his father, not since the day Walter had caused him to split his head open on the glass-top table. But things were changing. Rowan was changing.

"To what do I owe your new attitude?" Walter asked.

"The love of a good woman. And if she'll have me, I'd like to marry her."

"Then I wish you the best of luck," Walter said. "The constant fights with you have been exasperating, to say the least. And quite frankly, I have enough to worry about."

It wasn't exactly what Rowan wanted to hear, but it was a start.

"I never have liked drinking alone," his father said. "Why don't you have another beer? I know you've got a long ride back to your place, but you can stay the night in the guest room."

"I just might take you up on that offer." Rowan stood and glanced at the door. "Will you excuse me for a moment? I want to make a phone call."

"Sure."

Rowan wanted to tell Louanne that he was ready to face the future, that he'd tied up all those loose ends. And that even if the past couldn't be altered, a person's perception and attitude could be. Of course, he wouldn't discuss all that now. Not here. But he could hint at it.

And he could also hear the soft lilt of her voice.

He picked up the phone in the hall and dialed her number. As the line continued to ring with no answer, he grew concerned.

Where was she? Louanne never left the ranch.

He returned to the library, where he and his father continued to have a cautious, yet generic conversation. But off and on that evening, he kept trying to call Louanne.

And there hadn't been an answer, even long after she should've been home and in bed.

Was the phone off the hook?

An uneasiness settled over him. And he wasn't at all sure why.

Chapter Thirteen

Rowan woke before dawn and tried to call Lou-anne again.

There was still no answer.

He didn't know where his uneasiness came from. Was that what happened when a guy fell in love? He grew more concerned about his lover than himself?

Maybe so.

When Rowan went downstairs, he found Brenda bustling about the kitchen. She hadn't noticed him yet, so he watched her, a smile forming on his face, a warm glow in his heart. After her husband died, the Parks children became Brenda's life. And she was the only mother Rowan had ever really known.

At sixty-five, Brenda looked the same as she always had, although he suspected she'd shrunk a tad in height, if she'd ever actually reached the five foot mark, as she'd always claimed.

The scent of yeast and spice wafted through the room, as Brenda prepared a homemade cinnamon twist Rowan had always favored. She was a darn good cook, which contributed to her ample girth. But neither her age nor her weight stopped her from kicking up the heels of her sensible shoes, once the Parks kids moved out of the house and didn't need her anymore.

Rowan heard she was taking an aerobics class, answering personal ads for companionship and enjoying her golden years by traveling, taking cruises and seeing the world.

But when she was home, the Parks house was still her castle.

"Breakfast ready?" he asked.

Brenda turned and grinned, her pleasure at seeing him hard to ignore. "Rowan! You get over here and give me a hug, you little rapscallion."

Rowan chuckled and gave her a hug, her familiar embrace wrapping him in warmth, her lavender scent bringing back memories of her maternal love.

She patted his back affectionately. "It's so good to have you home."

"Wheelie," he said, using the nickname he and Cade had come up with years ago, "I love you."

She gasped, stepped back from the hug and grabbed his forearm. Her eyes widened, and her lips parted. "You've never told me that before."

No, he hadn't. He'd kept a lot of his feelings under

wraps. And when he'd come home to make things right, this was one of them. "I should have told you how much you meant to me years ago."

"I always knew, but it feels so good to hear you say it." Her eyes grew watery, and she swiped at them with the back of a plump hand. "I love you, too, Rowan. And in spite of your penchant for mischief, you've always held a special place in my heart."

Okay, so he'd said the words he should have voiced years ago and was glad he'd finally leveled with her, but that didn't mean he was comfortable with sappy stuff like that. He slid her a boyish grin. "Like I said, what's for breakfast?"

Her familiar laugh, loud enough to be heard throughout every estate in Pacific Heights, rang throughout the kitchen, making him feel more at home here than he had in years. "You sit right down and have a cup of coffee and a cinnamon twist while I fix you a hearty breakfast. Your dad left the morning paper on the table."

"Yes, ma'am." Rowan picked up the newspaper, glanced at the headlines, then scanned the front page. A picture of his father drew his attention.

Well, what do you know? The press was quick to report the news about the paternity results of the DNA test. They hadn't included a photo of the twins, which was too bad. Rowan knew what Tyler looked like, but he was curious about Conrad.

"Did you read this?" he asked Brenda.

She nodded. "And so did your father before he left

for the office. The papers don't take long to print what they consider sensational stories."

"You know anything about Tyler Carlton?"

"Not much. He's a detective."

Before Rowan could respond, the telephone rang.

"Will you answer that for me?" Brenda asked, as she whisked scrambled eggs in a glass mixing bowl.

"Sure." Rowan picked up the receiver off the wall-mounted kitchen telephone. "Hello."

The caller introduced himself as Tyler Carlton and asked, "Is Walter in?"

"This is Rowan. Can I give him a message?"

"I called to tell him that I'm sorry about the media coverage. I don't know how in the hell the press got wind of the paternity results. That wasn't my intent."

"The press loves a good story about this family." Rowan remembered his own scandal while in college and all the national coverage it had received.

"I'm not the kind of guy who likes to be front-page news," Tyler said.

"Neither is our father. By the way, I guess a 'Welcome to the family' is in order."

"I didn't expect any kind of welcome. Your dad will probably never get used to the idea."

"Hell, he's still getting used to the idea of having me in the family," Rowan said.

The men spoke for a while, then agreed to meet for drinks sometime.

"My best friend's brother, Mark Banning, is getting married this weekend," Tyler said. "So I'll be busy with that."

"And I'll be going back to Texas soon. We can talk about it more when I get back."

After they said goodbye and the line disconnected, Rowan held the receiver in his hand. He ought to call Louanne one more time. Something wasn't sitting well with him.

But when he dialed the number, the phone continued to ring and his uneasiness mounted. He couldn't put his finger on what had him on edge. It was more than missing her, more than just knowing that she and Noah were alone on the ranch.

His discomfort had begun with that phone call he'd received the evening before he left the ranch. Had it been a wrong number? A random call?

Or had hearing a man's voice surprised the caller? Had the man expected Louanne to answer?

Rowan's imagination kicked into high gear. Had it been Noah's dad calling to check up on his kid? To check up on Louanne?

No, the guy was dead. Louanne had told Rowan so. Of course, when he'd asked her how the man had died, she'd refused to talk about it.

Thinking the subject had been too painful he'd asked if she missed the man. And she'd said, "I don't miss him at all."

When Rowan had asked whether Noah's dad had seen his son, she'd told him no. And she'd admitted to not being sorry that the guy wasn't around to be a part of Noah's life.

He's not a nice man and wouldn't have made a good husband or father.

He's not? Present tense?

Okay, now Rowan's imagination was really going wild, and for no reason at all. Not really. He didn't have anything solid to go on. Just this rock-hard knot in his gut.

He'd half accepted the idea of Louanne having a form of agoraphobia. And he'd assumed she steered clear of the people in town because she didn't want them to know she'd had a child out of wedlock. But Louanne loved Noah. And he doubted she'd be ashamed of him.

Oh, God. Was she hiding out from Noah's father? Is that why she'd given up her dreams and become a recluse?

Rowan picked up the phone one last time and still got no answer.

Louanne might not be in danger. But he wasn't going to sit in San Francisco and ponder the idea while she and Noah were alone on the ranch.

Problem was, it was going to take him hours to get to Pebble Creek.

While Noah napped, Louanne took a basket of laundry outside to the clothesline, where Rowan's pants and shirts hung on the line, drying in the warm, summer breeze.

Rowan hadn't called yet. But then again, he couldn't have reached her. She'd forgotten to turn up the sound of the ringer until lunchtime.

The old adage said, "No news is good news." Still, if she didn't hear from him by this evening, she might give him a call. Curiosity and a growing need to hear the sound of his voice was making her stir-crazy.

A car sounded in the distance, and she turned to see who it might be. There wasn't anyone in the yard, so maybe the driver had merely used the Lazy B driveway to turn around.

An old crow landed upon a tree stump near the copse of trees that bordered the house and cawed. She turned again, glancing over her shoulder. An uneasiness settled around her, although she wasn't sure why. Just lonely and jumpy, she supposed.

As she hung the last of the diapers on the line, she snatched up the basket and headed for the house. Noah would be waking soon.

She wiped her feet on the mat in front of the service porch door, then entered. The house was quiet, which meant Noah continued to sleep. She had half a notion to check on him, to watch his peaceful slumber—something she always found comforting. But instead, she busied herself in the kitchen.

The screen door squeaked, although she didn't hear the door open or shut, nor did she hear the sound of footsteps. A cold shudder shimmied down her spine.

"Rowan?" she asked. Had he come home? Maybe he changed his mind and hadn't gone to San Francisco after all.

No answer.

And her baby was just down the hall. She picked

up the cast-iron skillet that rested on the stovetop, hoping it would work as a weapon, if need be, and proceeded into the living room with caution.

No one.

Had the squeaking door been her imagination? Or had the house settled? Maybe the wind had kicked up and blew it open, but that didn't seem likely.

She continued her slow, mindful search and headed down the hall, toward Noah's room. She needed to know her child was safe.

When she reached Noah's open doorway, she gasped at the sight of a man hovering over the crib.

A tall man in a tweed sports jacket and rumpled khaki slacks turned and faced her.

Richard had found her. And Noah.

Her heart dropped into the pit of her stomach.

For a man who prided himself on being neat and well dressed, he'd let himself go. His ash blond hair hadn't seen a comb in a while. And he needed a shave.

His blue-gray eyes narrowed. "Well, hello, Lanay. Or should I call you Louanne?"

She gripped the handle of the skillet, willing to use it as a weapon, if she had to.

Her first impulse was to ask what he was doing here, her second was to cry for help. But she did neither. She knew why he'd come, just as surely as she knew that no one would hear her scream.

Richard pulled back the edge of his jacket, allowing her to see the gun tucked in the waistband of his slacks. "If I didn't know better, Lanay, I'd think you meant to harm me. Why don't you put that thing down?"

The skillet wouldn't protect her from his bullet, if he meant to kill her. So she set the cast-iron pan on the top of Noah's dresser. Trying to add a touch of normalcy to the conversation, she asked, "Can I get you a glass of iced tea?"

He stepped away from the crib, away from her sleeping son, his hand on the butt of the pistol, his eyes aimed at her.

"It took some time to find you, since you apparently put a phony address through the entire college system. In Austin, I finally found someone who claimed to have known Tallulah Brown before she made it big." Richard smiled, but his eyes remained cold. "He still had her number, if you can believe that."

She didn't respond.

"The first time I called, a man answered. I'd thought it was a wrong number. But just last night, I heard your voice."

Her eerie intuition had been right. Richard had been the one who called.

"I had breakfast in Pebble Creek," Richard said, continuing the *normal* charade, "at a nice little place called the Bluebonnet Café. Folks in small towns are so much friendlier than those in the cities. And they're much more talkative than you."

She glanced at Noah, saw him stir.

"While seated at the counter, I chatted with a pleasant fellow who actually dated your sister in high school. He called her a tease." Richard's lips tensed, his gray eyes narrowed. "Like you."

Her heart threatened to burst free of her chest.

"I'm disappointed in you, Lanay. I thought we had something special." He tore his gaze from hers, then focused on the napping child. "How old is he?"

A wad of fear settled in Louanne's throat. She didn't want Richard to know the baby was his, although he surely suspected it.

Did she dare lie? Let him think she'd slept with someone else, adding validity to his accusations, and really set off his fury?

But she was afraid to lend fuel to his warped need to possess her and their son.

"How old is the baby?" he asked again.

When she didn't answer, he was across the room in an instant. He grabbed her by the arm, fingers pressing hard into her flesh, and twisted. "How could you have done this to me?"

She winced. "Done what?"

"I loved you, *needed* you. And you threw that back in my face. You left me. And for what reason?"

"My grandma died," she said, reiterating the lie she'd told him when she left. "And I had to come home."

"That's a lie. You ran away and tried to hide, but you underestimated me." His grip relaxed, yet she didn't feel safe. "And you weren't as clever as you thought."

She tried to pull away, and he jerked her. Hard. "You lied to me, time and again. And if that child isn't mine, I'll have proof of your infidelity."

When she didn't answer, he asked, "Who is that kid's father?"

"The man you accused me of seeing," she said, making a decision that might be her last. But Richard had never been a man's man. Had never confronted anyone who might prove to be a physical match. And her only hope to protect herself and Noah was to convince Richard he'd have an imminent fight on his hands. "And he'll be home any minute. You saw his clothes hanging on the line."

"People who love each other don't do that to one another, Lanay. They don't lie, they don't cheat and they don't leave."

Then he jerked her from Noah's room. When they reached the living room, his nails dug deep into the tender underside of her arm. There was no one to hear her, no one to come to her aid.

Unwilling to quietly submit and be his victim any longer, she grabbed the heavy, ornate picture frame from the lamp table and struck him in the head. Hard.

But not hard enough.

His eyes widened, rage brewing, as a trickle of blood slipped down his cheek. "You bitch." He doubled his fist and slammed it into her face.

The pilot of the jet Rowan had chartered out of San Francisco offered to land him at one of the smaller, executive airports in the Austin area, rather than have him face the hubbub at Austin Bergstrom International. But since Rowan had flown commercially to Frisco and left his Harley at a Park and Ride, that's where he wanted to return.

He wasn't looking for comfort or special treatment. He just wanted to get home.

Home.

Funny, how that run-down ranch felt like home. But it wasn't the house, the property or the rural atmosphere. It was Louanne and Noah who drew him to the Lazy B.

Rowan hadn't shaken the uneasiness he'd felt earlier, and in fact, it had merely increased.

Of course, there were a hundred reasons why Louanne might not have answered. The phone line, like everything else on the ranch might have just worn out. Or maybe she'd decided to go with Pete and Aggie. Heck, maybe she'd left him a note.

Still, he gunned the engine of his Harley and sped faster. When he turned off the country road and onto the drive that led to the ranch house, he noticed an unfamiliar car parked along the side of the graveled road. A blue sedan. Pennsylvania plates.

Had someone run out of gas? Gotten lost? Or had someone from her past wanted to make a surprise arrival?

Rowan's apprehension doubled, and to be on the safe side, he parked the Harley near the car, then hurried up the drive on foot. When he reached the yard, he heard voices coming from the barn.

"He's not yours," Louanne cried out. "Can't you get it through your head?"

A thud sounded. And then silence.

Rowan slipped around to the side of the barn and peered into the nearest window, his gaze hampered by years of dirt and grime. He caught a glimpse of Louanne, who'd been tied to a post in the barn. Her face had been battered, her nose bloodied, her lip split.

A man dressed in khaki slacks and a sports jacket stood near her, a gun in his hand. Noah was nowhere to be seen.

Desperate to save the woman he loved, Rowan slipped around to the back of the barn. He hoped the hinges on the back door weren't as loud as the ones on the front.

The back wall bore another window, just as dirty as the rest—maybe more so. He could make out a male form.

"You deserve to be punished for your deceit," the man told Louanne. "I had plans for my son. That baby should be mine. In fact, I'm not at all sure that he's not."

"Richard, please, try and be reasonable. Untie me so we can talk."

Rowan picked up a rock near the doorway with his right hand, then grabbed the worn, wrought-iron handle with his left. His muscles tensed, ready to spring into action in the biggest fight of his life.

Not willing to waste any more time, he chucked the rock diagonally through the window as hard as he could.

When the man turned to the sound of broken glass and the thud of the rock that hit the barn wall, Rowan rushed inside and leveled him to the floor.

A scuffle broke out, and he knocked the weapon from the man's hands. The gun skidded across the floor, as arms flailed, fists pummeled. But Rowan was no stranger to bar fights turned free-for-alls. It didn't take him long to silence the man with a blow to the head, knocking the fight out of him.

Rowan picked up the gun from the straw-littered ground, wanting to send the cowardly bastard on a bullet train to hell.

Instead, he untied Louanne and slipped an arm around her, the gun still aimed at the prostrate man on the floor. "Are you all right?"

"I am now that you're here." She touched a swollen eye and winced. "Oh, Rowan. I was so scared. I've got to go to Noah."

"Where is he?"

"Sleeping, I hope."

"Call the sheriff while you're in there."

She nodded, then limped into the house.

Thirty minutes later, Richard Keith was handcuffed and arrested for stalking, kidnapping and attempted murder. As he was led to a patrol car out front, he glared at Louanne, who held Noah in her arms. "Who is that kid's father?"

"I am," Rowan said. "I protect what belongs to me. And don't you forget it."

Rowan drove Louanne to the emergency room of a nearby hospital, not only to make sure her injuries weren't serious, but to document what Richard had done to her. He carried Noah in his arms and took charge—just like a devoted father and husband.

They still hadn't discussed the future, but Louanne was certain of one thing. She loved Rowan with all her heart, and she couldn't imagine raising Noah without him at her side, couldn't imagine spending another night without him lying next to her, his arms wrapped protectively around her.

She'd showered and shampooed her hair earlier, but that evening, after Noah had eaten dinner, Rowan insisted she soak in a warm bath. "To make you sleep better."

He'd been right. She did feel better.

She carefully dried herself, then put on her white cotton nightgown. As she stood before the mirror, she ran a brush through her hair, making it shine. But there wasn't much she could do about the black eye, the bruised and swollen cheek, the cut on her puffy lower lip. She looked like hell, probably because she'd been there earlier today. But something positive had come out of the frightening and painful experience.

Richard wouldn't be getting out of jail for a very long time. And he wouldn't be able to bother her again, to rob her of things like peace of mind and happiness.

As she entered the living room, she spotted Rowan on the front porch swing and joined him outside.

"Feeling any better?" His voice was soft yet husky, comforting, and he made room for her to sit beside him.

"Yes and no." The swing creaked and swayed when she sat. "I'm glad you came when you did."

"If I would have known about that bastard and his threat, I wouldn't have left you alone." He reached for her hand, threading his fingers through hers. "You've got to promise me something."

"What's that?"

"There won't be any more secrets between us."

"You've got my word." She had no problem making a vow like that. She wanted him to be honest with her, too. "I've never really had anyone in my corner before."

"Neither have I."

"I'm sorry for not trusting you," she said. "I should have told you about Noah's father when you asked."

"Just wait one darn minute." Rowan released her hand and caught her chin with the tip of his finger, turning her gaze to his. "Let's get something straight, honey. I have every intention of being Noah's father—whether you'll have me as your husband or not."

Her heart swelled to the bursting point, and tears blurred her sight. "I love you, Rowan. More than I'd ever thought possible. And I can't imagine anyone else being a father to my son."

Rowan slipped his arms around her, gently but firmly. "I love you, too. So what do you think we ought to do about that?"

"I'm not sure." She had a suggestion, but she thought he should propose the solution.

"It's taken me a long time to find love and a family of my own, and I'd like you and Noah to be a permanent part of my life." He brushed a gentle kiss across the tip of her nose. "I'd like to make things legal as soon as possible. How does a wedding in Las Vegas sound?"

"It sounds wonderful to me." She smiled, ignoring the sting of the cut on her lip. "Where would you like us to make our home?"

"As long as we're together, I don't care. If you'd like to live on the ranch, I'll set up my tools in the barn until I can build a permanent carpentry shop."

"The Lazy B has never held any real appeal to me," she said. "I don't need to stay here. In fact, I don't even want to."

"Then let's start fresh. We'll buy a little place in the country. I'll make furniture, and you can finish that novel."

A grin tickled her lip, causing the cut Richard had inflicted to sting, but she didn't let it bother her. The man she loved had just proposed, and the future lay before them, bright and promising. "Do you mind if we celebrate?"

"What did you have in mind?"

"I'd love to sleep with you tonight. In a bed."

Rowan smiled broadly. "There's nothing I'd like more than lying beside you all night long. And I'll try to keep my hands to myself."

"Why in the world would you want to do that?" she asked.

"Because you're hurt. And sore."

"I'll bet you'd be gentle." She stood and reached for his hand. "Come on, Rowan. Take me to bed."

Louanne led him into her bedroom, where they celebrated their love for each other. Rowan took her in his arms and tenderly brushed his lips across her brow, kissing each bruise that Richard had left on her—the ones on her body as well as her heart. And she pressed healing kisses on his heart and soul, as well.

Their joining was slow and easy, the passion building into the fire that blazed inside them. And as he entered her, she arched to meet him, giving as well as taking.

They reached the same mountainous peak, one that reached the heavens, and as the waves of pleasure encompassed them both, they took the first step toward a shared and promising future.

Man and woman, father and mother. Lovers who'd found forever and locked it deep in their hearts.

* * * * *

Don't miss the fourth book
in the thrilling continuity
THE PARKS EMPIRE
THE PRINCE'S BRIDE
By Lois Faye Dyer
Coming in October 2004
Available wherever Silhouette Books are sold!

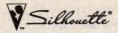

If you enjoyed what you just read,
then we've got an offer you can't resist!

Take 2 bestselling love stories FREE!

Plus get a FREE surprise gift!

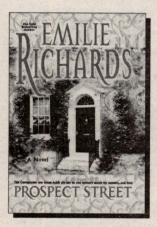
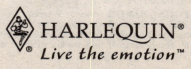

COMING NEXT MONTH

#1639 MARRYING MOLLY—Christine Rimmer
Bravo Family Ties
Salon owner Molly O'Dare vowed to never be single *and* pregnant.
That is, until a passionate love affair landed her in both of these
categories. The child's father—wealthy and dashingly handsome
Tate Bravo—insisted on marrying Molly. But she was determined to
resist until he could offer exactly what she wanted: true love.

#1640 THE PRINCE'S BRIDE—Lois Faye Dyer
The Parks Empire
Wedding planner Emily Parks had long since given up her dream
of starting a family and decided to focus on her career. She never
imagined that the dashing Prince Lazhar Eban would ever want
her to be his bride, but little did she know that what began as a
business proposition would turn into the marriage proposal she'd
always dreamed of!

#1641 THE DEVIL YOU KNOW—Laurie Paige
Seven Devils
When Roni Dalton literally fell onto FBI agent Adam Smith's table
at a restaurant, she set off a chain of mutual passion that neither
could resist. Adam claimed that he was too busy to get involved, but
when he suddenly succumbed to their mutual attraction, Roni was
determined to change this self-proclaimed singleton into a
marriage-minded man.

#1642 NANNY IN HIDING—Patricia Kay
The Hathaways of Morgan Creek
On the run from her evil ex-husband, Amy Jordan accepted blue-
eyed Bryce Hathaway's offer to be his children's nanny. This
wealthy single dad was immediately intrigued by the beautiful
runaway, but if he discovered that this caring, gentle woman was
actually a nanny *in hiding,* would be help her out—or turn her in?

#1643 WRONG TWIN, RIGHT MAN—Laurie Campbell
Beth Montoya and her husband, Rafael, were on the verge of
divorce when Beth barely survived a brutal train accident. When she
was struck with amnesia and mistakenly identified as her
twin sister, Anne, Rafael offered to take care of "Anne" while she
recovered. Suddenly lost passion flared between them…but then her
true identity started to surface.…

#1644 MAKING BABIES—Wendy Warren
Recently divorced Elaine Lowry yearned for a baby of her own.
Enter Mitch Ryder—sinfully handsome and looking for an heir to
carry on his family name. He insisted that their marriage be strictly
business, but what would happen if she couldn't hold up her end of
the deal?